Margaret Thomson Da
age of three, apart f
during the war. She is
author of some two
number of novels.

By the same author

In the Breadmakers trilogy

A Baby Might be Crying
A Sort of Peace

The Prisoner
The Prince and the Tobacco Lords
Roots of Bondage
Scorpion in the Fire

MARGARET THOMSON DAVIS

The Breadmakers

GRANADA
London Toronto Sydney New York

Published by Granada Publishing Limited in 1983

ISBN 0 583 13626 5

First published in Great Britain by
Allison & Busby Limited 1972

Granada Publishing Limited
Frogmore, St Albans, Herts AL2 2NF
and
36 Golden Square, London W1R 4AH
515 Madison Avenue, New York, NY 10022, USA
117 York Street, Sydney, NSW 2000, Australia
60 International Blvd, Rexdale, Ontario, R9W 6J2, Canada
61 Beach Road, Auckland, New Zealand

Printed and bound in Great Britain by
Cox and Wyman Ltd, Reading
Set in Times

In loving memory of my brother
Audley S. Thomson

Chapter 1

There was still unemployment and empty shops, but Duncan MacNair's bakery and general store had weathered the Depression and survived.

Women pushed in wearing aprons and slippers, or if they came from the maze of streets further along the riverside they arrived hugging heavy shawls around themselves, often with babies cocooned stiffly inside.

The traveller who shuffled through the open doorway of MacNair's, however, wore a long blue belted raincoat, underneath which his feet barely showed. The coat, shined smooth with age and years of carrying bulky samples, was topped by a milky-moon face devoid of any expression except resignation.

The shop bulged with people sweat-glistening with heat from the bakehouse at the back. Maisie the shop assistant was working at such a pace between the bakery counter at one side and the general store at the other, she was too breathless to talk.

But old Duncan MacNair, the master baker, ranted into his goatee beard as if all the customers were devils ganged up out of sheer badness to harass him.

The traveller manoeuvred his long raincoat among the hot flesh and, with a sigh, placed his case up on the bakery counter.

Feeling out his order book he began his usual monotone: 'Abdines, Askits, blades, bleach, Brasso . . .'

MacNair's bloodshot eye popped.

'I've no time for you today. Can you not see I'm busy?'

Well used to nobody having any time for him, the traveller went on with his list. 'Bandages, castor-oil and zinc, cough mixture, notepaper, french letters, pipeclay . . .'

'Beat it!' The womanish voice reached a top note that spurted saliva out.

'Sanitary towels, safety pins, Snowfire Cream . . .'

'It's the Old Govan Fair today,' Duncan howled. 'Did you not even see my horse out the front?'

'Christ, the Fair, I forgot!'

'Come on.' Two blotches of pride warmed old MacNair's cheeks. 'Have a look at the best dressed animal in the parade. He'll lift that prize again. By God, he will!'

Outside in Dessie Street, Sandy McNulty the vanman was chatting to Billy the horse. Sandy was so painfully thin it was as if a mischievous God in a cruel mood had caught him by the nose and feet and stretched him out of all proportion, leaving both nose and feet forever red and tender, and body without enough covering to keep it warm.

'You're a smart one, my Billy boy,' he was assuring the frisky, restless beast. 'There'll not be another horse in the whole procession to come near you.'

Old Duncan ignored him and addressed the traveller.

'Look at that!' He thumped a gnarled fist against the horse's rump, making it clatter its hooves on the cobbled street with indignation, and snort and toss its head.

'What did I tell you!' Sandy protested, grabbing the bridle.

A little crowd had gathered in Dessie Street to admire the horse. People going down the Main Road which cut across Dessie Street stopped to stare and others in the tramcars, trundling along the Main Road through Clydend to Govan Cross and further on into the centre of Glasgow, craned their necks round to keep staring.

Billy was a splendid sight and, judging by his proud prancing and the tossing of his head, he was well aware of his splendour.

Sandy had brushed and polished him with loving care until his red-tan hide gleamed. Even his hooves had been polished. A large scarlet and silver plume curled royally between his alert twitching ears; rosettes and flowers decorated his bridle; scarlet, silver and purple ribbons were plaited all over his reins and rippled from his tail; but the *pièce de résistance* was the magnificent saddle-cloth sparkling in the sun. Plush purple velvet was encrusted with silver and a many-jewelled design. The Dessie Street children were convinced that the fiery red and amber and emerald stones were real jewels and not coloured glass because rumour had it that, despite old MacNair's scraggy appearance and second-hand clothes, he was loaded.

Attempts had even been made to divest him of some of his wealth. The last try had been when a local gangster rushed into the shop brandishing a cut-throat razor and demanding all the money in the till. Old MacNair, outraged at the mere idea, had immediately screamed at him and chased him away down the street with a long butcher's knife lashing the air like a cutlass.

'I'll cut your bloody head off if I catch you, you cheeky big nyaff!'

Now he yelped at the traveller.

'Look at the float, too. Help me get the covers off, man, Don't just stand there like an accident looking for somewhere to happen!'

Between them, and to the mounting excitement of the onlookers hastily gathering in the narrow street between the high sooty tenements, they removed the covers from the four-wheeled vehicle standing behind Billy.

The crowd of neighbours – women in wrap-around overalls and slippers, some with masses of steel curlers in their hair, pale-faced men and little boys with skinny thighs in 'parish' trousers, girls bouncing up with heads straining – all jostled closer with loud ahs and ohs, inarticulate with admiration.

Bristly sheaves of corn hugged round the float. At the nearest end to Billy, a huge, flat wooden loaf stuck up displaying the words

MACNAIR AND SON
BREADMAKERS

'I'm going to sit up front with Sandy. Melvin will be in the back with the rest of them. They're going to be tossing pancakes as we go along and I've got hundreds of wee loaves packed in there to throw to the crowds. Christ!' The old man's excitement suddenly fizzled out and he nearly burst into tears. 'That bloody show-off of a son of mine'll be the ruination of me yet. You'd think I was made of money. This was all Melvin's idea. Hundreds of good wee loaves. Could you beat it?'

The traveller said nothing but looked vaguely impressed.

'He'll be wanting to pelt folk with my pancakes next. I'd better go and see him. He's through the back helping with the pancakes now.'

Knees lifting and cracking, he hustled back into the double-windowed corner-shop, punching customers roughly out of his way, and made for a piece of sacking that served as a curtain between the shop and the ill-lit lobby. The left-hand side of the lobby housed the lavatory and wash-hand basin. Next to the lavatory the side door led out to the close, and directly across from the curtain was the entrance into the white floury heat-haze of the bakehouse.

Melvin stood, tree-trunk legs well apart, one shovel-hand gripping white-aproned hip, bushy moustache bristling with concentration, neck muscles knotted, shoulder muscles bunched, arm bulging as he strained – ever-faithful to the rules of dynamic tension – to lift a Scotch pancake and imagine with all his might that it weighed half a ton.

All Melvin's fellow night workers, except Rab Munro who lived over in Farmbank, had been upstairs to their respective flats for a sleep and had returned to the bakehouse to help get everything ready for the Old Govan Fair.

A bald giant of a man, looking like an all-in wrestler with sweat splashing over his face, was bringing new batches of miniature loaves from the oven with the long handled pole or 'peel' and roaring in song.

The 'halfer', or apprentice, was over at the pie machine 'lifting' the pies.

Tam, another baker, his feathery white hair standing up on end, was swaggering along with more pancake batter for Jimmy the confectioner and Melvin, who, because of the special occasion, was helping him. Unlike Melvin and the other men, Jimmy always worked days along with his female assistant, Lexy.

Lexy nudged Melvin and laughed, making her own well-developed but softer flesh bounce and wobble.

'I bet you're dreaming about your new lady love. I've been hearing rumours!'

'She's got nothing on you, darlin'.' Melvin's free hand suddenly shot up and twitched over Lexy's full melon breasts, making her squeal.

Suddenly old MacNair's high nasal tones snipped through the hilarity.

'Stop your messing about, you randy nyuck! And what the hell are you playing at with that pancake? Anybody would think it was as heavy as an elephant, or you'd glued the bloody thing down. If it wasn't for Jimmy here, where would we all be?'

Jimmy cast a long-suffering glance towards the ceiling as he continued rapidly flipping over the pancakes. Only the other day MacNair had insisted he was a 'good-for-nothing young Dago'.

Tam the white-haired baker smacked and rubbed his hands then gave Melvin's back a punch.

'You were awful concerned about Rab that last time he was off work, eh? How many times was that you went over to Farmbank? We've heard about Rab's daughter. We've heard she's a beauty. Young, too. Sweet seventeen and never been kissed! Or is it sixteen? And a blonde as well. You'd better watch out for Baldy. He's a devil for blondes.'

Melvin scratched his moustache. 'She's a queer one but I'll soon knock her into shape.'

'You keep your hands off the girl or there'll be trouble. You're old enough to be her father. Where is Rab, anyway?' grumbled old Duncan. 'He'd better be on that float tonight with the rest of us. I don't care if the big sod's dying.'

'One thing's for sure, I'm a damned sight fitter than her father,' Melvin said. Then, shoulder and arm muscles bulging, he went back to his tussle with the pancakes.

Chapter 2

The Old Govan Fair was always held on the first Friday in June and dated back to the fifteenth century, when Govan itself was barely a village and Clydend had no existence at all.

It had been originally granted by ecclesiastical rescript and at one time was the occasion of annual festival and holiday when the local deacon was elected.

The village band turned out to play for the retiring deacon at his residence, and it was also the custom for the band to halt at each public house en route in order to serenade the landlord. He, in return, was expected to come out into the street with a bottle of 'the cratur' with which he regaled all the bandsmen. The result was that although the music had been distinct and lively at the beginning of the march it deteriorated into a mere confusion of hiccoughing sounds long before the journey ended.

The main function, however, was not to pay court to the retiring deacon but to elect a new one. After the solemn business of the election was over, the proceedings quickly gave way to jovial rejoicings. A procession formed and marched to the boundaries of the village carrying the famous 'sheep's head' hoisted aloft on a pole and gaily decorated.

The sheep's head with its shaggy hair and big curling horns had always been the emblem of the Burgh. Legend had it that, long ago before ships were built in Govan, a pretty girl had come to serve in the manse and a young man had begun to court her and eventually asked for her hand. The cleric put his veto on the alliance and refused the youth permission to continue seeing the girl. The young man nevertheless succeeded in carrying her off and, in celebration, or revenge, he cut off the heads of the sheep in the glebe lands of the manse and left these grim relics lying on the ground.

The villagers, siding with the young couple, took the choicest specimen of the sheeps' heads and did it honour publicly by carrying it on the Fair Day all along the village street to the ancient 'Ferrie Bot' hostel at Water Row, where they all got 'roarin' fou and unco' happy' drinking the health of the happy couple.

The traditional sheep's head was still carried but the procession had grown with the place. Govan had at one time been a village on the banks of the River Clyde, but over the years increasing industrialization exploded the once-peaceful water's edge with the endless clamour of the shipyards and the giant cranes crowding to reach the sky. Now, there were high honeycombs of tenement buildings behind the yards. Bustling shops with fruit and vegetables spilling out on to the pavements, draperies with dense doorways of hangers bulging with clothes. Dark brown, sawdust-floored pubs at every corner where money could be spent when men were working. When they were not, gloomy, dusty caverns of pawn shops with brass balls above where precious possessions might fetch a few shillings.

The roads of Govan formed the shape of a ladder, with the long, straight Govan Road nearest the Clyde and the more pliant Langlands Road further back. The rungs of the ladder joining these two main roads, from Clydend in the south to past Govan Cross at the City of Glasgow end, were – first – Burghead Drive, Holmfauldhead Road and Drive Road. At this point the ladder widened to encompass Elder Park with the public library at the corner. Then the rungs continued towards the Cross with Elderpark Street, Elder Street and Golspie Street. Next came Harmony Row with Burleigh Street angling off it into Govan

Cross. Helen Street went into the Cross too, like Robert Street which arched from it.

Splintering back from the Cross, right on the river bank in the space between Fairfield's yard and Harland and Wolff's, there was a huddle of short, narrow, dark and very ancient streets, like Water Row, clustering around the Govan Ferry and the Govan Wharf.

Like Clydend they, with their rich tapestries of characters, were part of Govan and the Bacchanalian mother city of Glasgow, yet communities on their own with their own city-sizes hearts, their own fierce loyalties.

The Old Govan Fair procession started at the marshalling point in Burghead Drive. All the floats gathered there prior to their triumphal progress from Langlands Road at Pirie Park, along Langlands Road and through the old Burgh.

Burghead Drive was electrified by noise and colour.

A huge crowd clamoured, laughed, chattered, squealed, heaved this way and that by desperate boiling-faced marshals fighting to make order out of chaos.

Spilling from both ends of the Drive were close on eighty decorated floats, motorvans and carts, unrecognizable in their gay dress. Horses were stampering, with whinnies and snorts, rearing at the excitement. Flags were fluttering; the noise of revving motor-bikes mixed with the ting-a-linging bells of flower-cycles. The Boys' Brigade, cheeky pill-box hats strapped tight under chins, were tippering drums. Heavy-jowled mustachioed police pipers were concentrating, tartan pipes wailing, screeching, squeezing under iron arms. Jarring jazz bands, with bearded wild-eyed maestros, thumped a bouncy New Orleans beat.

Further along in Elder Park another swarm of people waited impatiently, heads craning for the Govan Fair Queen.

A wooden platform had been erected and the Royal

Naval Volunteer Reserve (Clyde Division) Band was playing with great energy and enthusiasm.

The first car to arrive carried the convener of the Fair, and he welcomed the guests and ushered them to the dais. The guests included Govan's member of Parliament and other local dignitaries. There were also representatives from the local hospitals to whom all the money collected at the Fair was to be given.

As each succeeding car approached, the crowd, agog to see whom it contained, leaned forward expectantly, on tiptoe to get a better view.

At last the clop of horses heralded the mounted policemen who were preceding the 'royal' landau. Thousands of lusty cheers welcomed the policemen and the car.

The sleek black landau drew up and out stepped the Govan girl who was to be crowned this year's Queen, resplendent in white organdie lace and purple robes trimmed with ermine. She was followed to the throne by her four maids.

The convener gave a little speech reminding everyone of the unlucky ones who could not be here to enjoy the festivities – the patients in the Farmbank Infirmary, the Elder Cottage, Southern General, David Elder, Shieldhall and Hawkhead Hospitals.

'We would like,' he shouted from the roof of his voice to make sure he could be heard in every corner of the park, 'to bring as much comfort as we possibly can to these unfortunates and we are looking to the big-hearted people of Govan to rally round and give every penny they can manage.'

Pockets, bulging with pennies ready to fling at the floats, eagerly jumped and jingled.

'And now it gives me great pleasure,' the convener continued in a voice already cracking and getting hoarse, 'to ask Mrs Struthers, wife of our Medical Officer for

Govan, to crown Miss Flora Rattrey Queen of the Old Govan Fair.'

Mrs Struthers, flushed and pretty in a frothy confection of yellow hat, rose and the convener relaxed down in his seat, only to bounce straight up again, every nerve at the ready. His eyes bulged at the wolf-whistling multitude, and he gesticulated for silence with waving arms and thickly pursed lips.

Order was restored but the convener did not risk sitting down again. He hovered in the background strafing the crowd with sharp admonishing stares as Mrs Struthers lifted the crown.

'I now crown Miss Flora Rattrey Queen of the Old Govan Fair.'

With these words she laid the symbol of majesty on the Queen's head and cheering swooped upwards.

The Old Govan Fair procession was about to begin.

The streets were awash with colour. Red, white and blue Union Jacks of all sizes, and the gold and red lion rampant of Scotland, swayed and flicked and cracked. Streamers streamed rainbows, bunting puffed and flapped.

Melvin had instructed Catriona to secure a good vantage point on Langlands Road at the end of the park near the library.

'Make sure you come without your mother, mind,' he warned her. 'And as soon as the procession's over, I'll come back and meet you.'

It hadn't been easy getting out without mother because all Catriona's life Hannah Munro had kept a conscientious eye on her and had insisted on accompanying her everywhere. It made the situation doubly distressing that she had been forced to give a reason for wanting to go off on her own. Unpractised in the art of telling lies, she could think of no alternative but the truth. Her mother immediately tried to restrain her and lock her in the front room, but to miss the Govan Fair as well as a meeting with Melvin proved too much for even a person of Catriona's timid temperament.

For the first time in her life she mutinied, actively rebelled, fought tooth and nail in fact, and rushed sobbing but triumphantly free from the house.

All the same, she was glad when she met Norma, a neighbour's daughter, and they crushed together on the pavement's edge outside the park and danced up and down, giggling and squealing like children in eagerness for the procession to come.

Catriona's excitement at seeing Melvin was always sharpened by fear. He was an unknown (and now forbidden) quantity. She had not the slightest idea what was expected of her in speech or behaviour in any man's company and the extent of her newly-discovered ignorance appalled her. Melvin was her first male friend and she found herself, without warning, like the person in the experiment who is locked for days in the black-dark, silent, sound-proofed room, completely divorced from the normal stimuli of sight, touch and hearing, the measure, the criterion acquired through learning and experience with which to judge a situation and react with appropriate patterns of behaviour. Every time she was with Melvin, she was blind and deaf and alone.

'Here it's coming!' Half-laughing, half-crying, she clapped her hands.

'Here's the police!' A delighted yell broke out. At any other time such a cry in Glasgow would immediately disperse any crowd, clear the streets like magic, but on the day of the Old Govan Fair the City of Glasgow Police Pipe Band led the procession and a splendid sight and sound it was. Many a Glasgow villain's heart warmed towards it and they felt proud, and boasted at having been 'nicked' by one of the big 'Kilties'.

The cheeky swaggering skirl of 'Cock O' The North'

took command of the road. Pipers in the red tartan plaids and kilts of The Royal Stuart, giant men in bearskin headgear, short-stepping, kilts swinging, were in immaculate military order with each drone or bass pipe pointing up from exactly the same place on each man's shoulder.

Catriona felt so moved by the sight and sound of the pipe band she could have wept on Norma's shoulder. Emotion ranged free and, unused to the freedom, pride and happiness became distressing to the point of grief.

After the police pipe band came the sheep's head held aloft, then the Navy band, then the Queen's landau and the motorcade of guests. Then came another pipe band with a big mustachioed drum-major marching out front and tossing and twirling the mace with nonchalant panache, eyes glued straight ahead, not needing to watch the intricate manoeuvres of hand and arm, aggressively confident.

Then the decorated floats with motor-bikes weaving in and out of the procession, and in between the floats, too, bands and more bands until the whole of Govan rocked with sound.

And tenements towered above the procession and tenants were a crush of faces and arms and hands at every window and the sky became a chinkling, winking, sparkling copper-gold shimmer of pennies descending on to floats.

Catriona watched the big letters *MACNAIR AND SON – BREADMAKERS* come into view.

All the men on the float and the pretty bright-eyed girl were dressed in white trousers, white jackets, white aprons and jaunty white hats. Heads were tossing back, laughing, arms were jerking, throwing out, golden bread was pelting the crowd.

A tall young man, his curly hair blue-black against the white uniform, was tossing pancakes with intense concentration, flipping high, higher, bumping, reaching, always catching.

Catriona's gaze rested on him. Then she was startled by the unexpected pain of a crusty loaf flung by Melvin finding its target on the side of her face.

Chapter 3

'Leerie, leerie, licht the lamps,
Long legs and crooked shanks . . .'

The summer's evening closed its eyes, shutting out light. Black velvet darkness softly muffled sound, hid the crumbling stone of the Dessie Street tenements, the ugly carving on the walls, the litter, the dust, the chalked pavements.

A bottom-flat window was open wide and a woman leaned out on folded arms. A cluster of other women lounged outside, some shoo-shooing infants at the same time as chatting about the Govan Fair and everything that had taken place during the eventful day.

A sheaf of youngsters propped itself up in the gutter to watch the lamplighter raise his long pole to the gas-lamps all along the street. The children chanted their song to him but with weary voices dragging fainter and fainter.

'Leerie, leerie, licht the lamps,
Long legs and crooked shanks . . .'

The street took on a cosy hue as the leerie's pole, like a magic wand, touched each lamp, springing it into brightness that faded into a circle of flimsy yellow on pavement and road.

Behind curtain-closed windows people slept, peaceful in the knowledge that life continued. There was always a baby exercising newborn lungs somewhere, its screeching muffled by high buildings and hole-in-the-wall beds. Someone was always having a 'hing' out some window and there were always a few men leaning or squatting at street corners. Across the Main Road in Wine Row, the short street that ended at Clydend Ferry, the shebeens were supplying the winos with Red Biddy. The meths drinkers were down at the river's end, huddles of hairy spiders, not human, yet more pathetically human than anyone, hugging bottles deep in their rags, oblivious of everything except the individual world of fantasy to which they had retreated.

But in Dessie Street the bakehouse, the warm nucleus of life, was busy with breadmaking sounds as front closes puttered and hissed into flickering light and back closes became echoing tunnels.

Melvin had taken Catriona and Norma home. He had only succeeded in shaking Norma off for a few minutes in the park by dodging behind some bushes with Catriona firmly held in tow.

'If it's not your mother, it's your next-door neighbours!' he had hissed. 'I'm fed up with this. It's time we got married!'

'Married?'

'You heard what I said. It's time somebody cut your umbilical cord. Anybody would think you were an infant the way you're tied to your mother. Don't you know the law?'

'Law?'

'By Scottish law you can get married at sixteen without your parents' consent. Everybody knows that! I've got a palace of a house.'

'Have you?'

'I've got furniture, dishes, bedding, the lot. I'm a hundred per cent fit and I've got a ready-made son – my son Fergus, a grand wee lad. What more could any lassie wish for?'

A silence dropped between them. Through the bushes he watched, with mounting exasperation, Norma coming nearer.

'Well?' His eyes bulged down at Catriona.

'Have we known each other long enough?' she queried, really anxious to find out.

'Och, we'll have plenty of time to get to know each other after we're married. I'll be good to you, if that's what you're worrying about. I don't drink and I only smoke the occasional pipe. Here's Norma! Come on, come on, make up your mind, woman!'

Catriona was prodded into giving a harassed 'Yes' and Melvin irrevocably sealed the bargain by announcing the news of his proposal and acceptance to Norma who could hardly wait to tell the whole of Farmbank.

Now he sauntered into Dessie Street and up the close, shoulders back, big hands clinking coins in trouser pockets.

Already heat was blanketing out from the side door in puffs of white and beery fumes of yeast, and rolls were becoming golden, and bread steaming, doughy, sticking together, crusts floured on top.

Past the bakehouse door, he grabbed the iron banister and leapt up the stairs two at a time. Gulping in air, nostrils stretching, he paused at his own door on the first landing. Then as if unable to resist the challenge of the stairs he suddenly attacked the second spiral, pausing only for a minute between big Baldy Fowler's door and Jimmy Gordon's door before bounding up the last flight to the attics.

Lexy was a long time answering his knock and when she appeared her eyes were heavy with sleep and dark underneath where mascara had smudged against her pillow. She was absently rubbing the sides of her breasts making them quiver under her cheap cotton nightdress and the nipples tweak up.

'Ohi, in the name of the wee man!' she wailed, recognizing Melvin. 'Mr MacNair! I'd just went to my bed. Ohi!' Her hands flew to her face and hair. 'I was that tired, too, I didn't even bother washing my face.'

'You're all right.' Melvin strolled past her and into the house.

'Here, just a minute, Mr MacNair.' She followed him into the tiny camceiled kitchen, her bare feet slapping loudly on the linoleum.

'It's not time to start my shift yet. What's wrong? Has something happened?'

'No, not a damn thing. You're a fine figure of a girl, Lexy. Do you believe in physical jerks?'

Lexy gave an unexpected splutter of a laugh and Melvin glowered with annoyance.

'Nothing funny about that. I'm a great believer in exercise. That's why I'm so well-made.'

'I know, but could you not have told me that down in the bakehouse? Are you not working tonight?'

'Baldy knows I'll be late.'

'Want a cup of tea? The kettle's sitting on the side of the fire.'

His good humour returned. 'No, thanks, darlin'. It wasn't tea I come up for.'

She gaped at him, still glassy-eyed with sleep, but understanding splintered through with astonishment and another burst of laughter.

'Here, you're terrible, so you are!'

'Come on,' he grinned. 'I've seen Rab sneaking up here.'

'Rab's different. He's fond of me. And I'm sorry for him, so I am!'

Melvin put out his hands for her.

'All right, darlin', be sorry for me!'

'Away you go!' She ran light-footed across the room and clambered up into the high hole-in-the-wall bed, the exertion making her giggles become breathless.

Melvin followed at a more leisurely pace and, reaching the bed, stared at it with interest. He gave the mountain of mattress a punch, then heaved his solid bulk on top of it.

'Ohi! Get off, you daft gowk!' Lexy squealed. 'You'll burst my springs!'

'I've never been in a hole-in-the-wall bed before,' he admitted, settling down and loosening his tie, to the accompaniment of Lexy's piercing squeaks and her struggles to wriggle further up the bed and away from him. 'We've always had ordinary ones. It feels queer. Like being shut in a cupboard. But I suppose it's cosy in the winter tucked in here away from the cold draughts.'

'You're terrible! Away you go and try your tricks on with your own lassie!'

'Och, to hell! I'd need a tin opener for her!'

Lexy stifled a paroxysm of laughter with her fists but as soon as Melvin reached for her she punched him.

'You've a nerve! I told you – Rab's my man. He's real fond of me, so he is.'

'Rab's not your man and never will be. He's married and he's daft about his wife.'

Then, while her bleak smudgy eyes were still vulnerable with hurt, he gathered her to him.

Outside, the 'midden men', looking like coalminers with lights on their caps and string tied under the knees of their trousers, argued with one another about football. They filled their baskets with refuse from the overflowing middens in the back courts. Then, heaving the baskets over their shoulders, they returned, boots scraping and clanging, through the closes. The midden motor eased along at snail's pace while the men shook the refuse from their baskets on top of it.

A drunk with a bottle bulging from his jacket pocket lurched lopsidedly along the middle of the road singing, with terrible sadness and great enjoyment.

'The Bonny Wells o' Weary . . .'

A horse and cart rattled past him. Furniture and bedding and all the worldly possessions of an out of work family were roped on the cart. The family huddled on top, the children's heads lolling sleep-heavy, unconscious of the anxious world in which their parents could no longer pay the rent and had to 'do a moonlight'.

Over in Farmbank a lorry skimmed along, hugging the kerb, hissing water out, washing the streets.

Catriona lay curled in a ball in bed with 'Lovey', her pink hot-water bottle, clamped tightly between her legs. The violent scene of a few hours earlier when she had announced her engagement to Melvin was still flickering across her mind with the speed of an old-fashioned movie.

It had ended in a fight between her mother and father. Yet she knew that the question of her sudden decision to leave home and marry a man so much older than herself, and go and live 'in Clydend of all places', was far from finished. Her mother would nag on and on never-ending.

Catriona closed her eyes, tired beyond all measure of quarrelling and bitterness. She was thankful to be leaving it.

Chapter 4

Usually, when Catriona thought of marriage, she thought of a house. She imagined herself going around it dressed in a frilly apron and holding a feather duster out before her like a fairy queen's wand.

And when she strolled up the imaginary drive she admired the size of her dream house, the solidarity of it, and the purple clematis swelling lushly round the door.

It had a carpeted hall; everywhere there were carpets, warm, luxurious and muted, shutting out the draughts of the outside world.

Inside was all comfort and safety and pleasure to the eye; luxuries everywhere – paintings, standard lamps, bedside-lamps, quilts and counterpanes on the beds.

She visited it as often as possible and never tired, never became bored. There was always another cupboard, another corner she'd never noticed before, or an alteration to make, some improvement to attend to, a piece of furniture to change to a more convenient place or something to add to her stock of requirements. 'Good gracious!' She'd mentally throw up her hands. 'I haven't any fish forks and knives!'

The house was far more real than the flat above the bakery at Number 1 Dessie Street.

She could still hardly credit the fact that she was going to get married and live in a place of her own. Often she had prayed for someone – anyone – to come and whisk her away from Fyffe Street and change her life from misery to happiness, from bondage to freedom, but she had never dared to believe that her prayers would be answered.

'Where's your daddy?' Hannah dispersed Catriona's pleasant haze of thought.

'I don't know.'

'You don't know!' Hannah eyed her with disgust. 'Well, I know, all right. He's away hiding in some bar so that I can't get my tongue on him, that's where he is. But he's not going to evade responsiblity this time. I'll see to it. He's going to speak to that man because it's all his fault.

'If he hadn't been off work with his filthy dermatitis, that man would never have needed to come here to give him his wages. And if he hadn't come here he would never have seen you and all this trouble wouldn't have started. I've told your daddy already – Clydend's one of the toughest districts in Glasgow. I wouldn't live there and neither will you. Sooner or later he's going to speak to that man. But we're going to speak to him right now!'

'Speak to him?'

'Get your coat on.'

'But, Mummy!'

She followed her mother along the lobby and watched her dive into a coat and jerk on a reddish-brown felt hat.

'Get your coat on!'

'What do you mean – speak to him?'

'You're coming with me to that bakery in Dessie Street and you're going to tell that Melvin MacNair you certainly are not going to marry him.' Her stare pierced through the shadows into the hall-stand mirror so that she could tug at her hat with both hands to make it sit squarely and aggressively.

'The very idea! He's old enough to be your father!'

'But, I want to get married.' Stubbornness gave emphasis to Catriona's voice. 'And I promised.'

'Nonsense! Here, don't just stand there, child, get this coat on. You don't know what you want.'

She hustled Catriona into a coat and buttoned it up with strong, deft fingers. Having fastened the top button, she tidied down the collar, whisked out some of the long fair hair that had become tucked inside and smoothed it neatly over her daughter's shoulders.

Suddenly she stiffened as if something terrible had just occurred to her.

'He didn't touch you, did he?'

'Touch me?'

'Like I told you Bad Men do?'

Catriona's mind wrestled to bring to the surface and sort out tales of Bad Men jostling against girls coming out of cinemas or theatres and injecting them with concealed hypodermic syringes, then carrying them off to sell them in the white slave market.

Or Bad Men in cafés putting powder in girls' tea then secreting them away to lock them in backstreet rooms.

Bad Men that lurked behind bushes in the park or under the water in the swimming-baths. Everywhere there were Bad Men trying to touch girls and 'dirty them' and have their own way.

'I don't think he touched me.'

She stared up at the purple threads on her mother's cheeks and the large black pupils of her eyes.

'God will punish you, you know. He has strange and mysterious ways of working. He'll send his messenger of death during the night to take you away into the eternal darkness. Or someone you love will be taken forever from you. Or an accident will happen when you least expect it. He's watching you, Catriona – you'll be punished. Oh, you'll be punished.'

Before she realized what had happened Catriona was pushed and pummelled from the house.

Rab Munro had escaped and he flew along Fyffe Street, eyes popping, the early morning air catching his lungs like champagne. He had just done a hard night's work but he was not so tired that he had to lie in bed at home and listen to more of Hannah's ranting and ravings about Catriona getting married to Melvin.

Too restless even to wait at bus stops, he determined to continue on foot as far as the Main Road and then take the tram along to Dessie Street.

Secretly revelling in the exhilaration of the air and the victory in managing to slip out while Hannah's back was turned, he covered Fyffe Street with long rapid strides, head lowered, hands dug deep into pockets. Only once he'd turned the corner into Farmbank Road did his pace even out a little.

He stared around. Farmbank Corporation Housing Scheme was certainly a better place than Clydend for the wife and family to live, he thought with satisfaction. He hadn't failed Hannah there. He'd readily agreed that the MacNair building in Dessie Street was no place for her. No one could deny she was a good-living respectable woman. His mind turned over some of her qualifications for goodness with the usual mixture of pride, admiration, envy and sarcastic derision: President of the Women's Guild, member of the Farmbank's Help The Helpless Club, and Grand Matron of The Band of Jesus.

He crossed to the James Street Public Park side of Farmbank Road and tramped along close to the railings, big hands bunched, head sunk forward, arms squeezed forward as if holding up his chest. He could hear the soft rustle of the bushes and feel them reaching out between the iron to tug at his sleeve. His nostrils widened with the smell of them and the new-cut grass.

Often he escaped into this place. A wooded part at the other end was dark and jerky with squirrels. Without relaxing, his fingers poked at the corners of his pockets. Finding no nuts, he was both glad and disappointed.

Pain settled on his head and down behind his eyes, blurring them.

Without looking one way or the other he crossed James

Street, continued down Farmbank Road past the grey buildings of thc Farmbank Infirmary, across Meikle Street, then walked straight on until he reached the Main Road with its loud clanking and sizzling of tramcars.

He was thinking of bed, and Lexy. Sexy Lexy, they called her. Her bed, in one of the attic flats in the MacNair building, was wide and soft. He sunk into it in his imagination with a groan of relief. She'd be working now downstairs in the bakehouse, helping Jimmy Gordon cream and decorate the cakes, her spiky high-heeled shoes and bulgy calves almost completely hidden by the big white apron Jimmy insisted she tie round herself, but the apron and the long white coat did nothing to hide her hour-glass figure.

The rocking-cradle motion of the tram shuggled him off to sleep until the conductor's broad Glasgow bawl penetrated his snores and exploded in his ear.

'Hey, you! You get off at Dessie Street, don't you?'

He leapt spluttering to his feet, clueless about where he was and deathly cold.

'You doing an extra shift, eh?' The conductor grinned up from underneath a cap pulled down over his nose. 'Making your pile?'

'Sure . . . sure . . .'

He stretched an embarrassed smile at the conductor's ticket machine and poured himself off the tram as it trundled away.

The car stop was outside the high iron gates of the Benlin yards, and the equally high wall reared back along the Main Road as far as the eye could see, like a Scottish Bastille. Dirty newspapers flapped and skittered against it, and greasy fish and chip pokes moving more slowly and sporadically thumbed a nose at its bleakness, its harshness and its authority.

Past the stop, the wall turned into the part of Dessie Street that ended in the River Clyde and the Clydend

Ferry, and had become known locally as Wine Row because of the shebeens up the closes between the warehouses.

Trams clanked back and forward along the Main Road as Rab stared across at the MacNair building. It was on the corner of the Main Road and the other end of Dessie Street that led to a jungle of side streets and grey-black tenement houses. The building itself wasn't bad: old but solid, a roomy, double-windowed, double-countered shop with office, lavatory, store-rooms and bakehouse at the back and, above, four good-sized flats and two smaller attic flats. Old MacNair had a gold-mine here – no competition, nothing but tenements except the Anchor pub at the opposite corner, and then about half a mile down the Main Road the 'Tally's', and he supplied both with pies, and rolls and bread for sandwiches, cakes, cookies and scones. There was nothing up the other end either, except Granny's Café and MacNair supplied her, too, and of course the Ritzy Cinema, the local flea pit.

Sandy the vanman would be out delivering just now, his horse Billy clip-clopping, tail swishing, head up, ears cocked to listen for the Benlin one o'clock hooter that meant knocking-off time, a lively gallop to the stables, a big dinner and a long kip before brushing and grooming in readiness for the next morning.

Rab strode across the road, past the shop door and plunged into the first close in Dessie Street. He suddenly felt sick.

This had been his secret place. Shadow-dark even during the day, it titillated the senses with hot smells of new bread and mutton pies and spicy ginger cake from the bakery's side door.

Up the spiral staircase, round and round.

Melvin MacNair's flat was directly above the bakery.

Catriona would live here. The fool of a girl – the very

first man she'd ever known and she couldn't wait to sleep with him.

He fumbled blindly with the key of Lexy's flat, then made straight for her bed to lie head back, his face bitter and haggard. He didn't want Catriona to marry Melvin any more than Hannah did. Only he had more sense. He knew there wasn't a damn thing either of them could do to stop it.

He slept fitfully and wakened more ill-at-ease and guilty than if Lexy had been in bed, naked and pathetically vulnerable in sleep, beside him. It was as if some over-developed sixth sense warned him that Hannah was near.

Still cold and dazed with sleep and lack of sleep, he left the house in long reckless strides and clattered down the stairs, his boots sending hollow drum-beats up to the roof.

Until, unexpectedly, the ruddy-faced Hannah in war-like mood was blocking his path and he was clinging to the banister with the shock of seeing her there.

Catriona wept angrily beside her.

Chapter 5

The furnace heat of the bakehouse was immediately engulfing, and globules of sweat burst through every flour-dusted pore.

There were two entrances, one through the dough-hardened curtain of sacking from the shop-end – a few steps across the lobby that remained a slippery menace despite frequent moppings and scrubbings – and the other through the lobby side door that opened into the close.

The close and the stairs were washed regularly too but the flour had become part of the air, continuously moving and dancing, a white haze in summer sunshine against the landing windows, in winter an irritant to the throat and chest, scraping up coughs as folk puffed round and round the stairs.

It kneaded underfoot with the grease making a glassy paste to twist muscles and break unsuspecting bones. It lent even more variety to the diet of the rats that rustled deep in overflowing middens in the back court.

It fed the army of cockroaches that burst up from the heat of the bakehouse to cover the floors of the houses above like a busy blanket, a crawling coverlet that magically disappeared with the click of a light switch.

The humphy-backed cleaner who lived in one of the attic flats cleaned slowly and wetly, smiling to herself. Like the men who attend to the huge Forth Bridge, by the time she'd worked her way down all the stairs, through the close, the bakehouse, the lobby and the shops, the stairs were filthy and it was time to start at the beginning again.

Perhaps it was the frustration of this that made her the terrible torment, the practical joker of a woman she was.

Old MacNair had warned her that if one morc person was startled into screams by the sight of her kneeling in the shadows wearing a rubber mask, or if any more door-handles were found tied together or anything put through letter-boxes except letters, she would be finished for good, turfed out, lock, stock and barrel.

So the cleaner cleaned on and the flour thickened the air around her and her cloth slapped across the lumpy grease and her pipe clay squeaked as she decorated the grey stone with white intricate squiggles and patterns, and the heat crept up her back and the pungent smell of food made her mouth water.

The night shift had gone off. Big Baldy Fowler had stretched his muscles, rubbed his head in a cloud of flour dust, told the other bakers he was going for a kip, then gone upstairs as usual and made violent love to Sarah his wife.

Rab had buttoned his old raincoat over his sweaty shirt and flour-thick trousers and huddled into it, his face grey-gaunt over the turned-up collar, and, with only a tired nod, he'd slouched away to wait propped and heavy-eyed at a stop for a tramcar to Farmbank.

Melvin MacNair had carefully cleaned the two Scotch ovens with the scuffle, a long shaft or pole with a sack hanging on the end, a job he had always insisted on doing himself. Then he had hung his aprons in the lobby, washed himself in the lobby sink, changed his shoes, brushed himself down very carefully to remove even the slightest suspicion of flour, even brushed his hair and his moustache, donned a sports jacket and cap and gone smartly upstairs.

Only old Tam was left from the nightshift. He folded up the morning paper, flapped it on to the bench, scratched through his wispy white hair, then stretched luxuriously. The scraggy little body in the blue and white striped shirt with the tightly rolled-up sleeves lifted for a second out of the big white apron then shrunk down inside it again with a sigh of satisfaction. This hour, after the night's work and before he went upstairs to face his wife and daughter, was to be savoured to the full. He had relished his breakfast: a big mug of strong sweet tea, a meat pie and a couple of hot rolls oozing with butter. He had enjoyed every item of the paper from the front-page headlines to the small printed sports results at the back.

Now his bright pearl-button eyes twinkled around. Jumping to his feet he rubbed and smacked his hands together, his gorilla arms developed out of all proportion to his undersized body by years of chaffing and kneading up the dough.

'Going to the match, son?' He grinned at Jimmy the confectioner who was leaning over and staring very seriously into the mixing machine.

'Sandy was asking,' Jimmy replied. 'He's got a couple of tickets.'

'Old MacNair gave me one.'

'Gave?' Deep-set eyes under jutting brows flashed round at him. 'Old MacNair never gave anything. Either he sells at a profit or there's strings attached.'

'Oh, I can't complain, son. He's supplied me with many a good feed without knowing it.'

'We work hard for all we get. And he gets most of it back for rent and food. Talk about daylight robbery!' Jimmy's words spattered out with machine-gun rapidity. 'Have you heard that song about the company store? It could be our signature tune.'

'Don't bother about me.' With a laugh he gave his hands another smack and rub. 'I've a lot more to worry me than old MacNair's baps. Anyway, son, you're awful young and you've a lot to learn about folk. There's a lot worse than old MacNair going around.'

'Your Lizzie, for instance. I know what she needs. A nice big fella!' Lexy flung her loud undisciplined voice at him as she passed with one of the cake tins she had been filling.

'Who needs a nice big fella?' Sandy the vanman, a giant bean-pole with red hair, a red nose and chronically sore feet, tiptoed gingerly into the bakehouse, his lips blowing and puttering, a habit he'd acquired while curry-combing his horse to keep the dandruff from flying into his mouth and up his nose.

'Tam's lassie.'

Lexy clattered the cake tray down beside Jimmy then returned to the other end of the bench, buttocks and bosom bouncing. 'How about you, Sandy?' Winking a heavily mascara'd eye at the vanman she patted the white cotton turban that covered the steel curlers in her hair. 'Or are you daft about me, eh?'

'I've enough to contend with, with my horse!'

Chortling to himself Tam went out into the lobby that separated the bakehouse from the front shop. The side door was open and, as he was untying his apron, the halfer appeared, his freckled face creased in his usual grin, the scone or padded bonnet that protected his head against the weight of the boards pulled down over his eyes.

'Hi, Tam!'

'Hi, son!'

Hitching up his trousers the young halfer marched past him and into the bakehouse.

Tam looped the tape halter of his apron over a peg before leaving by the side door.

'I'm away!' he called. Into the close with a jaunty jog trot and up the spiral staircase.

Next to Melvin's, his door was the cleanest on the stair. Every inch of it was exquisitely polished and the brass name plate and letter-box and keyhole glittered bright yellow.

'Just let me catch any of them saying I don't keep a clean house,' Lizzie never tired of repeating. She had a bee in her bonnet about folk gossiping about her behind her back or trying to get at her in one way or another.

Carefully he rubbed his knuckles on his jacket before knocking exactly in the middle of the door. Then he waited, small on the doormat, faded and floury, praying that Lizzie wouldn't accuse him of spilling the white powder around on purpose.

Sarah Fowler was thirty-five years of age and despite her blonde hair and her slim figure she looked every minute of it. Easing herself downstairs she clutched at the iron banisters. Pain dragged at her lower back, belly, buttocks and thighs with exquisite precision. Her patchily made-up face had long ago set in a twisted pattern of suffering that could not untwist even when she smiled and she smiled more than most.

Reaching the first landing she rested thankfully between Melvin's and Tam's doors. Then, thinking she heard a sound from the latter, her nerves twitched into action and forced her feet down the rest of the stairs at twice her previous speed despite the pain. Anything was more bearable than a tirade from Lizzie – anything, she hastened to correct herself, except the bagpipe moaning of Lender Lil, the mother-in-law to beat all mothers-in-law.

She stopped again in the close to get her breath back, shoved her message basket further up one arm and hugged her coat more tightly around herself.

She was beginning to dread the mornings. First thing Baldy did when he came off work from the bakery was get into bed beside her and have his loving. Not that she was complaining. She was grateful for and flattered by Baldy's attentions. It wasn't his fault that she'd had one miscarriage after another until her inside felt red raw.

That wasn't the only thing she felt. She had become so tired, so continuously and indescribably tired, even coming downstairs to the shop was like an expedition to the other ends of the earth. And the cold . . . oh, the cold! She closed her eyes, her scalp contracting, her icy fingers bending stiffly inside two pairs of gloves.

'Are you all right, hen?' Sandy McNulty came out of the side door as if on stilts, a bread-board squashing his ginger hair down.

Immediately Sarah's face crinkled into a grin.

'Och, aye. Just feeling the cauld as usual. It's ma watery blood. Got any guid stuff to spare?'

'We're two of a kind, hen. See this red conk? Everybody thinks it's a boozy yin. Booze be damned, I keep telling them. I'm just bloody frozen!'

'Ah think we'll have to emigrate, Sanny.'

He winked at her as they emerged together into Dessie Street, he with his stiff bouncy lope as if he were trying to avoid stepping on white-hot coals and she with her slippered feet and small tired shuffle.

'Just you say the word, hen, and ah'll be there.'

'Away with ye!' She poked him in the ribs before turning to go into the shop and although it was only a gentle shove it nearly over-balanced his bread-board.

Poor Sanny, she thought. She wouldn't have him in a gift. She felt keenly sorry for the vanman with his thin blood and red nose and the agony he suffered with his feet but she wouldn't exchange him for her Baldy, not in a thousand years.

There was nobody like Baldy. He was a real hefty hunk of a man who looked more like an all-in wrestler than a baker. He hadn't a hair on his head and he'd always been the same, with skin as smooth and shiny as a baby's, but muscle-hard as if crammed with rocks underneath. No one had ever dared to torment him about his hairlessness. At school he'd sorted things out to his liking right from the start by beating up his fellow pupils in the baby class as a warning of what *would* happen if they even thought of tormenting him. But he allowed them to call him 'Baldy' because he'd never been called anything else.

Still smiling, Sarah pushed open the half-wood, half-glass door of MacNair's Bakery and General Grocers.

Being the foreman baker's wife gave her a special status here.

Already the shop was busy and her tired eyes lit with pleasure at the sight and sound of so many familiar people. Carefully she shut the door. Gratefully she savoured the heat of the place as it wrapped lovingly, comfortingly around her.

Old Duncan MacNair, no longer spending his nights in the bakehouse but working from nine to five or six in the shop instead, was taking his time serving at the counter, his few grey hairs carefully parted and greased down over his head, his straggly moustache and goatee beard wet and drooping at the edges. He wasn't that old, of course, only about sixty-five, and he had vivid blue and red veined cheeks, and glittery if somewhat watery blue eyes to prove it. He could be quick when he wanted, rheumatic hands clenched, elbows bent, boots lifting and clomping like Sandy's horse; but this morning he did not want to and Maisie his assistant was being forced, much to her annoyance, to speed up her pace.

'Oh, come on, Duncan, man!' a customer tried to chivvy him on. 'We'll still be here when the hooter goes and nothing ready for our men's dinner.'

Duncan's words came from his nose, not his mouth.

'It'll not take you long to fry your sausage and open your can of beans.'

'You mind your cheek. I'm not Rab Munro's wife, remember.'

'Rab Munro's wife?' Sarah's small rusty voice echoed over her shoulder. 'What's she got to do with it?'

'She was in here arguing the toss with old Duncan. But

I'll not argue with him. I'll be over that counter and chug the beard off his face.'

'Ah thought Rab's wife never came over here.'

'No, we're not good enough for her nor her blondie-haired daughter. She was trying to put a spanner in the works and stop the girl and Melvin getting married. Old Duncan chased her, didn't you, you auld rascal? I heard she went upstairs though.'

The first thought that leapt to Sarah's mind was that her husband had a weakness for blondes. Wasn't that why, no matter how tired she felt, she never failed to bleach her own hair? As soon as the brown roots began to appear she conscientiously attended to them.

A pulse twitched and leapt about her face and she hoped nobody could see it.

'Blonde, did you say?'

'Aye, long it was. I think thon hair must be natural.'

Lines of strain pinched Sarah's skin.

If only she had been able to give her man the wee laddie he wanted. It was right and proper that a man should want a son.

She felt ashamed – especially after all her man had done for her. Where would she have been, what sort of life would she have had without him? A bastard, brought up in a single-end – a dismal self-contained room – by a drunken granny, homeless when the old woman died and the factor put someone else in the house – where would she have gone but on to the streets?

That's what her mother-in-law always said.

The danger now lay in being ill and a nuisance to Baldy or being ill and having to leave him to go to the hospital.

A man needed to have his loving regular.

And then there was the worry about money, too. Baldy never complained but the expense of her being ill was terrible.

'Pretty, too, ah'll bet,' she quavered, her smile at its weakest.

'Not half!' The other woman unwittingly piled on the agony. 'No make-up or anything either, just a wee, long-haired bairn.'

Suddenly Duncan MacNair banged a gnarled fist impatiently on the counter.

'Come on, come on,' he ordered in his high-pitched nasal tone. 'What do you want? Let's have it!'

'Cheeky old rascal!' The customer plumped her message basket on top of his hand making him yell with pain. 'I don't envy that girl coming here. If she doesn't watch out she'll have this one to contend with as well as the other.' She suddenly bounced with laughter, and straining round to Sarah she added, 'He's fit for anything. And you'd better watch your Baldy, hen. He's a great one for the blondes is Baldy.'

'Aye!' By some miracle Sarah found herself laughing instead of weeping. 'He's an awfi man!'

The house was cold with quietness when she returned upstairs. And the coldness and the quietness made the house grow and made Sarah shrink; her slippered feet quickened their shuffle across the hall, pulled as if by a magnet to her retreat beside the kitchen fire.

The fire was not long lit and smoke spiralled straight up, suddenly to bend and collapse, flutter and puff outwards. Huddled dull-eyed in her chair Sarah watched it. A mouse in the cupboard behind her nibbled tentatively, delicately, then, thinking the house must be empty because of its stillness, it began scraping and clawing and gnawing with reckless abandon.

Sarah had drifted away to her youth: perched on her granny's bottom-flat window-sill across the road, her skinny legs swinging, her short cotton dress covered by one of her granny's long cardigans instead of a coat, she breathlessly admired the boys playing football.

Old MacNair's shop door served as one goal area, her granny's close the other.

Dessie Street echoed to bursting point with male yells, oaths, criticisms of play and desperate instructions.

'Tackle him! Don't let him through . . .'

'Clear it! Clear it!'

'No goal . . . no goal . . . it wasn't off!'

If a goal was scored in old MacNair's doorway it had the added excitement of one of the boys, usually Baldy, having to swoop into the shop to retrieve the ball and shoot out again with old MacNair hot on his heels screaming for the police.

And when the police, in the form of Constable Lamont, materialized (usually from the bakehouse where he had been enjoying a jam doughnut and a big mug of tea), the boys scattered and disappeared like cockroaches and Sarah scrambled down off the window-sill and hared up the close to the cries of protest from women having a lean out their windows above.

'Och, they were no doing any harm, so they weren't! How do you expect the Rangers and the Celtic to get any players if you'll no let them practise in the street!'

Baldy had eventually got a job at MacNair's and flung himself into the flour of the bakehouse with every bit as much energy, noise and enthusiasm as he tackled everything else.

One night in the bakehouse, after a bear-hug behind the flour sacks in the storeroom and a kiss that tasted of hot cross buns and had the squelchy sound of the dough-mixer, she told him that the doctor said she was expecting and for the baby's sake they would have to get married.

Baldy hadn't batted an eyelid.

'Aye, as soon as you like, hen. There's plenty room round at Ma's.'

Ma meant Mrs Fowler or Lender Lil as she was more commonly known because she was Clydend's money-lender. She did not have an office. All her business was done at her flat in Starky Street and there was a stream of people lapping in and out of Lender Lil's all day.

She was continually complaining about them and when Sarah moved in as Baldy's wife her resentment increased.

'Oh, yes,' she said with heavy sarcasm. 'Everybody lives off me around here, so why shouldn't our Miss Sweeney?'

'Ah'm not Miss Sweeney. Ah'm Mrs Fowler,' Sarah stubbornly insisted. 'And you shouldn't be keepin' Baldy's wage packet now. Baldy's my man. He should be handing his pay over to me. Ah'm his wife.'

After her miscarriage she persuaded Baldy to leave his mother's and take the house in Dessie Street, and his mother's complaints instead of ceasing became worse.

'Fancy, after all the sacrifices I've made for him, after all I've done, after keeping him for years while he served his time in that baker's, he ups and leaves me before I've time to get a penny-piece back. My only son. Little did I think my Baldy would ever do a thing like this to his mother. Of course it's not him, the big fat fool! It's you and well I know it, Miss Sweeney! You've tricked my boy into marrying you, now you're making sure you gets your hands on all his money.'

Often her harangues ended in floods of tears, but Sarah felt sorry for her. She suspected the older woman must be very lonely. Lender Lil maybe had diamond rings and gold watches and quite a bank account with interest money but she had very few if any real friends.

Her sympathetic feelings towards Mrs Fowler however did nothing towards weakening her claims on her husband. Baldy was her man and the house in Dessie Street was their home, and she thanked God for them both, not Mrs Fowler.

But now, with the news that another woman was coming to live on the stair, she felt heavy with secret hopelessness.

She had been young and bonny once and full of life and loving. She had even once had long fair hair. She remembered brushing it and tying it back with pink satin ribbon the day that she and Baldy got married.

She was suddenly agonizingly aware of the change in herself, of energy and eagerness drained away, the dewy wonder, the vulnerability, the excitement of youth dried up and toughened.

The more she thought of the newcomer to Dessie Street, the more her mind shrank away from the idea.

Like a mirror to the child she could be no more and could never have, Sarah did not know how she could bring herself to look at Catriona, and dreaded the ordeal of seeing her as she had never dreaded anything else before.

Chapter 6

The staccato stutter of the Benlin riveters filled to bursting point the whole Main Road and Dessie Street and all the streets in Clydend with a fiendish metallic noise that echoed all over Glasgow, even drowning the rumble and clanging of the tramcars

The people in Dessie Street had learned to live with it, to ignore it, to adapt their outside voices to broad, lusty bawls accentuated by elastic mouths that looked as if they were trying to make lip-reading as easy as possible for the deaf folk.

Women leaned out of windows and shouted pleasantries to each other and exchanged titbits of gossip. Little girls in the dusty street below squealed and giggled and teetered and tiptoed about in their mother's high-heeled shoes and too-long dresses and held on to huge-brimmed, feather-trimmed hats. Others were lost in rapt concentration, their eyes glued to a fast bouncing ball.

'One, two, three a-leary . . . four, five, six a-leary, seven, eight nine a-leary, ten a-leary postman!'

One child was crawling along the pavement intent on chalking in as big letters as she could stretch to: 'Alice Campbell loves Murdo Paterson'.

Big boys and wee boys were racing and slipping and dribbling and kicking and shouting and fighting, playing football.

Upstairs in Number 1 Dessie Street Mrs Amy Gordon, widowed mother of Jimmy Gordon the confectioner, snoozed in her rocking-chair beside her kitchen fire.

Sometimes at moments like this she thought her husband was still alive. She would waken, startled into awareness by the sound of the front door, a rush of joy bringing his name to her lips. And then in the heart-rending minute as she remembered, the world emptied. She was alone. Seven long years he had been dead yet her subconscious mind, her unconscious heart still refused to accept it.

He had been a kind and loving husband, a conscientious if somewhat strict father, and a good hard-working baker for MacNair's although he'd never got much thanks for it; a big bully of a man like Baldy Fowler was thought much more of in that place. The bakery had killed him; the long night hours, the heat, the extreme change of temperature outside that the body never had time to adjust to, the heavy lifting and handling, the breathing in of flour dust through the mouth, the nose, the lungs and every open sweaty pore.

They'd vowed that Jimmy would never have to follow in his father's footsteps and encouraged the lad to stay on at school. They'd even dreamed of seeing him at university.

Jimmy had an intensely studious and searching mind. He was always experimenting with things and asking questions and he soaked up books, any kind of books, at a truly bewildering rate. He worked his way through the nearest library at Elder Park in no time and was soon spending hour after hour in the Mitchell Library in the city.

'It's the most marvellous place, Mum,' he kept assuring her. 'They've even got a music room there.'

It worried her how he lay reading in bed till all hours in the morning and then emerged, white-faced, to sit with his dark eyes still glued to a book all through breakfast, or at least until his father came in and snatched the book angrily from him.

'Can you not strike a happy medium? No good can come of going to such extremes.'

Her husband had been sorely tried with Jimmy's

piano-playing as well. First the hours of laborious practising: the nerve-twanging scales, up, up, up, up, up, up, down, down, down, down, down, then the stumbling melodies, the suspense-filled pauses as Jimmy struggled to find the right chord.

'Is that you, son?' she called towards a sound in the hall, her rocking-chair squeaking forward.

Her answer was the strangely haunting notes of Sibelius's *Valse Triste* issuing faintly from the front room as if Jimmy were playing the piano miles and miles away.

She got up to make him a cup of tea, wishing he'd play more modern cheery stuff but nevertheless tum-tumming Sibelius and discreetly conducting with plump, ringed hands.

She sighed, but a smile deepened the creases round her mouth and eyes. He'd be sitting through in the front room now, covered in flour from the top of his curly head to the toes of his working shoes but not in this same world as her carpet and cushions.

The music gained in strength yet the gentleness of her son's fingers touched and stirred unknown levels of feeling. Her whole being was gathered up and carried along and swung into sadness with such poignancy that she stopped, tea-pot in hand, lips quivering.

Jimmy had had a rheumatic heart when he was a child and it still worried and distressed her. The doctor had said Jimmy was a fine big lad and he had youth on his side. His heart would heal and despite his excitable temperament he'd be all right, she would see.

Every night in her prayers she asked God that this should be so. 'Please, God, make my Jimmy all right.'

She made the tea, poured some into a cup, milked and sugared it and carried it carefully before her from the kitchen.

Outside the front-room door she waited automatically for the *Valse Triste* to stop, not daring to spoil the perfection of it. She made a strange and incongruous picture standing in the shadows of the hall, a little round barrel of a woman with grey-gold hair, a brown and green wrap-around apron and a cup of tea in her hand; while all around her swirled the music of the gods, quickening, dancing, saddening, pausing, swooping, gentling, gentling, until softly it faded away.

Jimmy's attention jerked as soon as his mother entered the room.

'You old rascal!' He grinned at her. 'Is this you spoiling me again?'

'Here you!' Laughing she handed him the tea. 'I'll have less of the "old"!'

He didn't want the tea. She always put far too much milk and sugar in it, but she was watching him, hands clasped over aproned waist, eyes eagerly waiting for him to enjoy it.

'Slàinte Mhath!' He swung the cup high as if it were filled with champagne then downed it in one go.

'Oh, my!' His mother radiated happy laughter and was a joy to see. 'You're an awful laddie!'

Affection for her surged through him and he just checked himself in time from flinging his arms around her and hugging and kissing her. It was unmanly to be emotional. At least it was unmanly in Scotland. Probably it was quite the reverse in countries like France or Italy. Which proved how ridiculous the whole thing was. Only a matter of social convention. It certainly wasn't a God-made rule. God, if there were a God, had given emotions to men as well as to women.

He wondered if other men felt as he did. Were they, too, isolating themselves on self-made islands of restraint?

'That was grand,' he lied, winking at her. 'You're the best tea-maker in Glasgow without a doubt, without a doubt.'

He preferred coffee every time. He enjoyed going up to

town on Saturdays to buy a half-pound of the real stuff. The old polished oak shop in Renfield Street – with its overflowing sacks of beans and crystallized ginger in jars richly painted with Chinese dragons – had a grinding machine that produced the velvet smell of coffee as well as the smooth brown powder. A hundred delicate aromas floated in the shop, and together formed a warm drug cloud to anaesthetize and titillate the senses.

He lingered there, savouring the sight, the sound, the smell of the place for as long as possible, happy to pace around waiting while other people were being served, then happier still to burst into eager conversation with the old man of the shop. The old man always seemed genuinely pleased to see him and they spoke about new blends and methods of percolating, and little tricks like adding a pinch of salt or mustard; it was as if no one had been in the slightest interested in coffee all week until he had come in.

The old man gave him pamphlets to study and Jimmy in turn searched out books from the libraries and the book-barrows on the history of the coffee-bean and the use of coffee, and the coffee-drinking habits of people all over the world, and he loaned them to the old man.

It was a fascinating subject.

'Get changed now in case somebody comes in.' His mother's voice broke into his thoughts.

'Is the water hot enough for a bath, do you think?'

'Saints preserve us, you had a bath last night and the night before, if I'm not mistaken.'

'Don't tell me the boss is charging us for hot water now? Measuring it out, charging us so much the gallon?'

'Och, of course not, there's plenty hot water.'

'Well, well, then?' Black brows pushed up, dark eyes filled with fun.

'But Friday night's bath night. Everybody takes their bath on a Friday, son.'

'And Monday's washing day?'

'That's right.' Her round apple face shone with pleasure again. 'And Tuesday's the ironing.'

'And all the time you have a renegade son, a terrible deserter of tradition.'

'Och, you're an awful laddie. Away and have your bath if you want to. But I've never heard the likes of it in my life.'

'You're the best mum in Glasgow.' He stretched up from the piano stool, massaging and exercising his fingers.

She shook her head at him but her hazel eyes were soft.

'Away and take that floury apron off in the kitchen.'

'Your word is my command, my command, Mother!'

He gestured for her to go through the door first. As she passed him, small and plump and dear to him, her head nowhere reaching the height of his shoulders, he couldn't resist the temptation to touch her and the touch immediately sprang into a passionate bear-hug that triggered off laughter and squealing as he swung her round and round the hall, not putting her down or setting her free until they'd together crashed noisily into the kitchen.

'Saints preserve us! Behave yourself, you cheeky young rascal. What'll the neighbours think? What a terrible carry on. You're an awful wee laddie.'

'Wee, did you say?' His handsome young face twitched mischievously. 'Wee, did you say, Mother?'

Tidying back stray wisps of hair and brushing the flour off herself Amy gazed ruefully up at him. 'No, you're no a wee laddie any more, are you, son? One of these days you'll be leaving your old mum to get married. Oh, here!' Her face suddenly alerted, remembering. 'You'll never guess who I had visiting me.'

Jimmy untied his apron, unbuttoned his white coat and stood naked to the waist, intent on stretching and massaging his shoulder muscles.

'Not Lizzie again. The old story, was it? What a good

mother she'd make for Fergus? What a good wife she'd make for Melvin MacNair? She has as much chance of marrying him as I have of playing the piano in St Andrew's Hall.'

Amy screwed up her face. 'God forgive me, Jimmy. I'd like to be kind and civil and act as a Christian woman should but I'm sorely tried with her.'

'When have you been anything but kind to Lizzie, Mother?'

Amy shook her head, then, remembering again, she brightened.

'Och, stop putting me off what I was going to tell you. You're such an awful blether nobody else can get a word in edgeways. It wasn't Lizzie. It was Mrs Munro.'

'Mrs Munro?'

'You know, Rab's wife. She's the Grand Matron at the meeting – the Band of Jesus. She's president of the Women's Guild as well, and dear knows all what. Although she's quite a young woman. She can't be much more than forty. Well, maybe half-way between forty and fifty. A fine-looking woman. She does a lot of good work, that woman, and, oh, I was fair upset.'

'Hold it, hold it!' Jimmy held up his hand. 'Just a minute. Why were you upset? Who upset you?'

'Well, you see . . .'

'Sit down!' He hustled her over to the rocking-chair. 'You just tell me all about it.'

She smiled up at him, eyes twinkling.

'I will, son, if you give me half a chance. It was nothing to do with me really, except that I was coming up the stairs with my messages and just as I reached the first landing and stopped to get my breath back, I heard raised angry voices from Melvin MacNair's house. Then suddenly the door burst open and out stumbled a wee fair-haired lassie and Mrs Munro punching her between the shoulder-blades to help her on her way.'

'Grand Matron of the Band of Jesus!' Jimmy's lip curled with distaste.

'But it was so unlike Mrs Munro to be violent like that. Punching the bairn sore she was. But she explained it all to me later, poor soul. She was so overwrought and upset she just didn't know what she was doing. I had her up here for a cup of tea and she rested until she felt better.'

'What about the child? She was the one getting hurt and upset.'

'Well, as it turned out, she isn't as young as I thought. I thought about thirteen or so. She just looks like a wee school-bairn. I can quite understand her mother getting all angry and upset about what Melvin's going to do.'

'What's Melvin going to do? What do you mean?'

'That wee lassie's the one he's going to wed.'

'My God!'

He could not help laughing.

Chapter 7

The Band of Jesus was having a special meeting in the front room. The proper meeting hall was in town in Dundas Street, a forbidding Victorian building of sooty black stone above the entrance of which a neon sign made a startling contrast, with bright busy letters telling the people of Glasgow that Christ died for their sins.

Special meetings of the Matrons, however, were held in the front room. The opening hymn wailed loud and long, some voices strong, others continually stumbling.

Catriona sat perched on the edge of the chair at one side of the living-room fire, her thoughts rapidly chasing each other. Her father filled the chair opposite, overflowed it, a gaunt silent mountain of despair staring helplessly at nothing, swamped, slumped, round-shouldered, long arms and square hands dangling.

Catriona felt as if there were a big placard hanging round her neck, shouting to the world in foot-high letters, IT IS ALL MY FAULT! She had not only been the cause of increasing her father's miseries but of her mother's obvious worry and distress as well.

There could be no getting away from the truth of what her mother said. If she had not agreed to marry Melvin MacNair, none of this would have happened.

First the embarrassing scene in the shop, then the anguish of seeing her mother, trembling and breathless, climbing the high stone stairs, hat slightly askew, hair-pins escaping unheeded from the bulky bun of hair at the back of her head.

'You wicked, wicked girl!' she kept repeating, puffing for breath and voice jerking near to tears. 'I don't know how you can do this to me, your own mother, After all I've done for you too. After all the sacrifices I've made for you.'

Melvin had taken a long time opening the door and when he did appear he wasn't the dapper smiling man that they expected. His eyes had shrunk and become red-rimmed. He was needing a shave and his normally smooth, wax-tipped moustache stuck out like a bushy old brush. He stank of sweat, and, horror of horrors, he stood there for anyone to see in nothing but his pyjamas. The blue-striped trousers, by the look of things and the way he was holding them bunched forward in his hands, had no cord to hold them up and were an obvious, terrifying and hypnotic menace to both Catriona and her mother.

'I was in bed!' he accused. 'But come in.'

They remained rooted to the doormat, their eyes as one pulled along by his bare-footed, trouser-drooping stomp across the hall. Reaching his front room he had suddenly noticed they weren't beside him and twisted round, one hand clutching his pyjamas, the other pushing open the room door.

'Come in, if you're coming.'

Afterwards Catriona became convinced that her mother would never reach the end of her harangue about him.

'I've never seen such a disgustingly vulgar man. He's not modest, Catriona. He's a vulgar and immodest man. How can you have even thought of a man like that? You! A well-brought-up, well-protected, well-sheltered girl like you! How could you have thought of that man?'

Catriona no longer knew what to think of Melvin.

She hoped the meeting would be a short one. No chance of bed until the Matrons of the Band of Jesus left. They would be sitting stiffly-corseted and barrel-bottomed on the bed-settee.

Once, after a particularly long session, not of the Band of Jesus but the committee of the Help the Helpless, she'd burst out: 'Thank goodness they've gone! I've been dying to get to bed for hours.'

'How dare you, you impertinent child!' Ruddy cheeks had purpled with anger. 'This is *my* home and this is *my* room and this is *my* bed-settee. *Nothing* here or anywhere belongs to you and never you forget it. Every stitch of clothing you wear, *I* paid for, every crumb of food that goes in your wicked ungrateful mouth, *I* bought!'

Not that Hannah had many worldly goods herself. She believed it her Christian duty to give everything away. Rab had two locked drawers in the bedroom to protect his treasures against his wife's generosity. Catriona's clothes and possessions were kept in a suitcase behind the settee but Hannah had long since wrenched the lock apart so Catriona had not Rab's enviable good fortune. Long ago she'd abandoned any idea of possessing real things. Her mother had got her hands on every single item from the dearly prized and jealously guarded bangle, a Christmas present from Uncle Alex, to her Sunday silk knickers.

As far back as Catriona could remember, Hannah had always loved to quote in a husky dramatic voice: '"Do not lay up for yourselves treasures on earth where moth and rust consume and where thieves break in and steal, but lay up for yourselves treasures in heaven, where neither moth nor rust consumes and where thieves do not break in and steal. For where your treasure is, there will your heart be also."'

At other times she'd straighten her shoulders and raise her strong chin and look the fine figure of a woman that she was and make the impressive pronouncement: '"Therefore I tell you, do not be anxious about your life, what you shall eat or what you shall drink, nor about what you shall put on. Is not life more than food, and the body more than clothing?"'

But they'd all have to eat something and wear something at the wedding. That was one of the subjects under discussion at the Band of Jesus meeting now. Someone, it seemed, had offered the loan of a wedding dress.

'You *want* to marry me, don't you?' Melvin, the front of his trousers still puckered up in his hands, had asked.

She'd nodded wide-eyed.

'O.K.,' he said. 'As soon as possible, eh?'

She'd nodded again as if, her mother later accused, he had hypnotized her or she was a puppet with him jerking the strings.

'And we'll make it a quiet affair, eh?'

Another movement of her head with her hair slithering forward and her eyes clinging to his unshaved, unwashed face.

'Nod, nod, nod,' her mother said. 'Like a gormless dumb donkey!'

The hymn singing stopped and now there was the drone of the Lord's Prayer. Automatically Catriona's hands clasped on her lap.

'"Our Father which art in heaven, hallowed be Thy name. Thy Kingdom come, Thy will be done . . ."'

'*Her* will, she means!' Rab sighed.

Catriona's eyes sprang open.

'What did you say, Daddy?'

He sighed again. 'Oh, never mind.'

The fire was dying in the hearth. Wind sang a melancholy tune in the chimney. Catriona's attention wandered round the room. An ancient railway-station waiting-place with limp cotton curtains, dark brown linoleum, a scratched wooden table, a few wooden chairs.

A memory of Melvin MacNair's house eased cautiously into her mind but guilt and fear flicked it away. Hastily she concentrated on Norma Dick next door. It would be nice if Norma could get married. What a lovely bride she would make walking down the aisle, a white veil frothy and spreading to vie in generous length with the long glistening train of her ivory silk brocade dress.

Norma would love to have a house of her own, full of things of her own, things like cushions and carpets and ornaments and . . .

'Catriona!' Her mother's voice exploded through the living-room door, and forced Catriona to her feet.

'Come through here at once and say thank you. Mrs Campbell's brought the wedding dress.'

Big women, fat women, double-chinned bewhiskered women, spread themselves in a circle round the room.

Smiling at everyone, like a performer acknowledging applause before doing a turn, Hannah prodded Catriona into the centre.

'Look at the nice dress Mrs Campbell is giving you a loan of. Say thank you like a good girl.'

'Thank you,' Catriona muttered, eyes down, not daring to look at anything.

'Mrs Campbell,' Hannah said at the same time, 'may the good Lord bless you, you're far too kind.' Then to Catriona, 'Don't just stand there, dear, hurry through to the bedroom and try it on.'

The dress had once been beautiful but it was now yellow-tinged with age and musty with moth balls. Catriona unrustled it from its wrapping paper and held it against herself without enthusiasm. There was a veil, too, limp and grey and sad-looking.

She put them on, then was hardly able to credit the humiliation of her reflection in the long wardrobe mirror. Little girls playing out in the street dressed up in their mothers' old clothes had looked better.

'It's no use,' she told Hannah, who appeared in the bedroom to circle her, muscular arms folded across her broad bosom. 'I'm too wee for it.'

'Beggars can't be choosers! It'll do very well. Come on through and let the ladies see you.'

'I can't do that!' Her voice raised incredulously. 'To be seen in your wedding dress before the wedding is bad luck.'

'Being seen in your wedding dress isn't what's going to bring you bad luck, my girl. Melvin MacNair's your bad luck.'

'No, please, Mummy. I read in a book. It's a bad omen.'

'Come on! Hold it up in case you tramp on it.' Hannah spoke at the same time as Catriona. Always, even after she'd asked her daughter a question, she never paid the slightest attention to the girl's voice.

Shame at her appearance, as well as fear, made Catriona dig her heels in, close her eyes, and stiffen her back when her mother pulled her.

Her mother let go. They both turned to speechless wax models. It was Hannah who recovered first.

'Honour thy father and mother,' she said and pointed dramatically towards the door. 'Go through there at once! No daughter of mine is going to break one of God's commandments. You've sinned enough as it is. He's watching you, Catriona. God misses nothing. Everything, every unkind, selfish thought, every cruel disobedient act, He takes note of and adds up for the terrible Day of Judgement when you'll stand before Him to await your final punishment. But make no mistake about this, Catriona, you'll be punished here, too. For every sin you're guilty of, there's a punishment.'

Her brown eyes acquired a faraway glaze and her mouth drooped at the edges with the weight of her bitterness. 'Your disobedience, your ungratefulness, your wicked selfishness will be punished. After all I've done for you, this is what I get. I nursed you and protected you and wrapped you in cotton-wool as a child and wouldn't ever let a draught get near you. I wouldn't allow you to play with other children in case they hurt you or contaminated you with their germs. Nobody could have had a stricter Christian upbringing. I've gone out to work since you've grown so that you can stay in the house all the time and I still look after you and watch over you as conscientiously as I did when you were a baby. And this is all the thanks I get. This is all the thanks.' She heaved a big shuddering sigh. 'You leave me!'

Chapter 8

It was more like a funeral-day than a wedding-day, Rab thought as he hitched his trousers up, fastened his braces then buttoned his fly. He went through to the living-room struggling irritably with his back stud.

Hannah was still sitting over the fire, chair jammed against the fender, big flat feet splayed out inside the hearth, skirts pushed up, legs wide apart, palms nearly up the chimney. She hadn't done her hair yet and it flowed over her shoulders and down her back like a girl's, a river of rich burgundy, its fruity glimmer heightened by the flames of the fire.

There were times, and this was one of them, when Hannah exuded sensuality.

Forgetting his irritation and leaving his still-white collar dangling, he gently laid a hand on her shoulder, and felt the gloss of her hair and the firm warm flesh. He longed to bend over her and slide his hand down over her bulbous breasts, and his breathing immediately became noisy, but with a quick disdainful jerk of her shoulder Hannah knocked him away.

'Have you no shame? Even on your daughter's wedding day, can you not think of anything else?'

She got up, bumping and crashing the chair aside, and began with brisk bitter movements to twist and pin up her hair. Peering at all angles of her reflection in the mirror above the mantelpiece she elbowed him out of the way.

'A lot you care about her, of course. The only person you care about is yourself.'

'What are you on about now?' He tugged furiously at his collar. 'You stupid fool of a woman.'

'May the good Lord forgive you for saying that, Robert, because I'm no fool and don't you forget it.' She faced him. 'I'll find out exactly why you were coming down those stairs at Dessie Street, and why when you saw me there you went as white as a sheet with guilt and nearly fainted.

'Guilt?' He raised his voice to a roar, fighting his collar now, avoiding his wife's eyes like the plague and hating himself for his lack of courage. 'Fainted! You're as mad as a hatter, woman. I never know what you're raving on about.'

'You were supposed to be home in bed, weren't you?'

'I told you, you fool! We've been over all this a hundred times before.' He sneered his hatred at her. 'I went back to see Francis MacMahon. He lives in one of the attic flats. So does his mother when she's not doing the scrubbing. So does his brother. So does his sister Maisie when she's not serving in the shop. Francis works in the yards. He promised to get me paint. I just wanted to remind him. That was all!'

'That was all?' Hannah faced him. 'Bad enough even if that was all! Don't you dare bring any stolen property into my house.'

'*My* house!'

'Oh, be quiet. I know who lives up there and it's an absolute disgrace, a young girl like that living in a house by herself. It's just asking for trouble and as long as there's wicked men like you going around, she'll get it!'

Unexpectedly Rab won the battle with his collar and sighing with relief he reached for his tie.

'If it's Lexy Brown you're referring to, she was downstairs working in the bakehouse all day.'

Depression swelled up like a pain in his chest and he sighed again. It would have been all the same if he had been at Francis's. She still wouldn't have believed him.

'I'll find out what's going on.' His wife's voice pushed

close to him. 'I had enough to contend with that day with that girl and the MacNairs, but after this business is over with that girl today, I'll be down there at Dessie Street again and with the good Lord's help I'll find out exactly what's going on!'

His tie fixed, Rab wondered why he was all dressed up. Then suddenly he noticed Catriona sitting waiting and remembered what 'the business' was with 'that girl' today.

'Is that her ready?' he queried incredulously.

'So you've taken an interest at last, have you?' Hannah plumped hands on hips and surveyed both husband and daughter. 'You're a bit late, are you not?'

'Whose granny dug that up? For pity's sake, Hannah, could you not have done better than that?'

'Could *I* not have done better? Oh, that's just like you, that's you all over. From the moment I found out about this awful business I've been trying in my own humble way to do my best for that girl. And I've been trying to get you to help, but would you, would you? Oh, no, not you! You were too tired. All you wanted to do was to shut me up and whenever my back was turned sneak out of this house and away to Dessie Street. And don't tell me you went trailing back there after doing ten hours' night-shift just to get a pot of paint from Francis MacMahon!'

'But look at her!' Rab said helplessly.

'If you'd taken the slightest interest in your own wife and family, if you'd given me extra money, I might with the good Lord's help have been able to buy her a new dress. But oh, no, not you. All you're interested in is that demon drink. And, of course, *you know what*!'

'I feel like a drink now,' he said, still staring at Catriona. 'By God, I do!'

'May the good Lord forgive you, Robert, for taking His name in vain. It's wicked, especially in front of a child.'

'A child?' Rab's voice gained in strength again until it

worked up to a howl. 'If anyone's mad in this house it's you, you fool. She's not a child any more. She's getting married!'

'And whose fault is that? Who's to blame for that child getting married?'

'It's no use talking to you.' He lunged away in disgust. 'I'm away out.'

'What?' Hannah gasped in genuine astonishment. 'You're supposed to take her to the Hall.'

Already he was in the lobby and grabbing his jacket.

'I'll take her when I get back. She's not due to leave for another hour yet.'

Out before Hannah could run to stop him. Across the road like a bird. Along the street, swooping, swerving, crashing among people.

In at last, dry-mouthed, pop-eyed, to a pub called The Wee Doch and Doris.

It was the twelfth of July and all over Glasgow, from Govan to Springburn, from Gallowgate to Partick, from Cowcaddens to Gorbals, Orangemen and their families were gathering for the Orange Walk.

Sitting alone in the living-room at the back of the house, because her mother had left for the Hall and her father had not yet returned from the pub, Catriona thought she heard a band. Hitching up her dress she ran through to peer out the front-room window.

Farmbank Lodge was swinging noisily along Fyffe Street on the first lap of their march from Farmbank through Clydend on to the centre of Glasgow to mass together with all the other lodges from the various parts of the city and then onwards in a huge drum-beating, flute-tootling, accordion-twisting, bagpipe-screaming, high-stepping, swaggering parade to one of the public parks where they ate like horses, played boisterous games, cheered speeches and listened to the bands.

The fiery-haired, fiery-faced leader of the Farmbank Lodge was well out in front and thoroughly enjoying himself – elbows out – four prancing steps forward, four prancing steps back as if he were doing a barn-dance. Big white gauntlet gloves swallowed up the sleeves of his jacket, and the long pole of the standard he carried was secured in a white leather holster strapped round his waist. Other people were carrying flags and banners, one orange silk one stretching the whole width of the parade and held aloft by a man at either end.

The leader's standard was of royal blue velvet fringed with gold and he sported a fancy purple and orange sash over his Sunday suit. In the middle of the standard an orange-cheeked picture of King William curled and furled and flapped about in the breeze.

The flute band at his back was giving a high-pitched excited 'Marching Through Georgia', and the leader, like the followers of the band, was singing with great bravado and panache:

> 'Hullo! Hullo! We are the Billy Boys.
> Hullo! Hullo! We are the Billy Boys.
> Up tae the knees in Fenian blood, surrender or ye'll die,
> For we are the Farmbank Billy Boys!'

Catriona had forgotten about the Orange Walk. Now she realized what a problem it would be for a car to reach Dundas Street until the Walk was over. She would never arrive at the Hall in time even if her father managed to come back in a fit state to take her.

It never occurred to her to feel angry, only guilty at keeping Melvin waiting. The noise, the movement, the excitement of the procession was infectious and, lifting her veil, she pressed her face close to the glass in case she might miss anything.

The men and the boys followed the band then came the women, the girls and the smaller children, all wearing their best newly washed and ironed clothes, some with fancy blue sashes looped over their shoulders, some with sparkling white, others with vivid orange.

Quite a few of the men and some of the women too were fast becoming completely carried away, jigging about wildly, hands high in the air, heughing at the pitch of their voices, dancing their own riotous version of the Highland Fling.

The drummers, sweat glistening over their faces, used every ounce of strength and energy, especially as they passed the Chapel of Saint Teresa. The drums got big licks then, and teeth gritted with the effort, and muscles ached and sweat poured faster. Tum – tari – um – tari – um – tum – tum, louder and louder until heads reeled and swelled with the noise. Tum – tari – tum – tari – tuma – tuma tum!

At last, the end of the procession – the skipping, giggling, strutting children – turned the corner into Farmbank Road, leaving Fyffe Street comparatively silent and deserted. Only Rab Munro was left taking the whole width of the pavement. His big gaunt figure had not enough flesh on it to fill his suit, his shoulders were bunched forward, his hands delved down into his pockets, his eyes were earnestly struggling to see the pavement but he was stumbling then suddenly spurting and lurching forward at such a lick he hadn't a chance to focus on anything.

Catriona was waiting at the door.

'Daddy, come on quick! Splash your face with cold water. The car will be here in a minute.'

'Aye, all right, hen.' He leaned a heavy arm round her shoulders. 'You're Daddy's bonny wee lassie, eh?'

'Oh, come on, Daddy.' She had to turn her head away from the hot sickly blast of whisky and beer.

'Anything I can do for you, hen, you've only to ask. You know that, eh?'

'I know. I know, but please hurry up.'

'It's an honorrarr . . . Marriage is an honrr . . . honourable estate. Did you know that, eh? Did you know that, hen? I'm telling you marriage is an honourar . . . honourrarr. Mummy's a bonny lassie. Always was. Always was.' He sighed. 'I'd never allow anyone to say a word against her. She's a wunnerful woman, wunnerful, wunnerful woman.'

'Daddy, please.' With a struggle, because she wasn't much more than half his size, she aimed him for the kitchenette and lurched along with him at an uneven rapid pace towards the sink.

Without a murmur of protest he allowed her to bend him over and wash and dry his face. The cold water did nothing to warm the grey lantern jaws and the blue-tinged eye sockets. It only dampened his enthusiasm down to a tearful moan.

'A wunnerful, wunnerful woman and it's true, perfectly true, what she says. I'm a heavy cross for her to bear, so I am. I have faults, so I have. Your daddy has faults, hen.'

'You're all right.' Suddenly Catriona felt weepy herself.

She thought she heard the screech of a car drawing up at the close. Sure enough there followed the clatter of a man's boots, then a loud rat-tat-tat-tat-tat on the front door.

'Daddy, that's the car. What'll I do?'

He straightened back his big bony shoulders.

'You'll take Daddy's arm and Daddy will lead you to Melvin.'

Peering down at her, he swayed forward again.

'You're happy, aren't you, hen? Tell me everything's all right, eh?'

She nodded and looked away.

'Have you the pennies for the scramble?'

All the children who were left in the district had gathered round the big black Co-operative car. They raised a hearty good-natured cheer when Catriona and Rab appeared, and milled around, jumping up and down and shouting, 'Hard up! Hard up!' and, 'Mind the Scramble, mister!'

Somehow, they managed to get safely into the car, bang the door, wind down the windows and spray out clinking, sparkling pennies which were immediately pounced upon by the screaming children. And the children were left a writhing knot of arms and legs on the pavement as the car moved away.

By the time it joined the Orange Walk the Farmbank Lodge had met up with Makeever Lodge, the Clydend Lodge and the Govan Lodge and the procession was four bands and a good two thousand strong. Every other person was wielding, waving, swishing banners, the sky was crowded with jostling, jumping colour.

Govan boasted a pipe band with a tiger-skinned drum-major. Makeever had accordions, Clydend a mixture of raucous brass instruments being played with swollen cheeks and enormous gusto, and all the bands including Farmbank Flute were concentrating on different tunes and even the echoes of the tunes overlapped and clashed with each other. From somewhere in the far distance the joyous bouncy strains of 'Scotland The Brave' joined the cacophony of sound.

The car slowed almost to a standstill.

'Would you look at the crazy devils!' Rab raised his shaggy brows and flung a look out of the window without moving his head or the big bony body that had sunk wearily into his suit. 'It was the Irish that started all this. They came over here looking for food and jobs and brought with them their ignorant bigotry. The Irish Lodges come over now to keep it going, pouring off the boats at the Broomilaw like mad dogs rarin' for a fight. Listen to them!'

Catriona nervously eyed the scene outside.

'I'm a Loyal Ulster Orange Man just come across the sea
For dancing sure I know I will please thee.
I can sing and dance like any man
As I did in days of yore
And it's on the Twelfth I love to wear
The sash my father wore.
For it's old but it's beautiful
And its colours they are fine,
It was worn at Derry Okrim,
Enniskillen and the Boyne.
My father wore it as a youth
And the bygone days of yore
For it's on the Twelfth I love to wear
The sash my father wore!'

'Why do we let them in?' Catriona asked, alarm heightening her voice.

Rab let out a roar of laughter.

'Why do we let them in!' He shook his head, making a lock of prematurely grey-streaked hair spread untidily across his brow. 'That's a good one!' His square hand thumped over her knee. 'Glasgow welcomes everybody, hen. Did you know that Glasgow was called the friendly city?'

Outside someone roared:

'King Billy slew the Fenian crew,
At the Battle o' Byne Watter,
A pail o' tripe came over the dyke
An' hut the Pope on the napper.'

'Will they be all right?'

'Who, hen?'

'The Catholics.'

'Of course!' her father scoffed, jerking his head towards the crowd outside. 'They're just out for a good time like at Hogmanay or a sail doon the watter.'

'But there's fighting in town, I've heard.'

'Och, there's fighting every Saturday night and oftener. Don't worry, nobody's going to go barging into houses and dragging out Catholics, if that's what you're afraid of. Once they get a drink tonight they'll fight anyone who wants to fight. It won't matter a damn whether they're Catholics or Hottentots. Most of the time they'll be sparring with themselves.'

'The Twelfth of July,' someone bawled in broad Glasgow vowels, 'the Papes'll die!'

'Silly fool!' Rab mouthed dourly as he sank further back into the depths of the car seat. 'The Raffertys upstairs are Catholics.'

'Are they?'

'Sure! And the best of luck to them! Who cares!'

Chapter 9

A grey and white haze had settled over everything in the Fowler kitchen. Ashes were heaped in an old enamel basin on the rug in front of the fire, and the dust from the ashes hadn't been swept or washed from the tiled surround, and Baldy's floury footprints had hardened on the rug and all over the linoleum. The previous night's newspapers spilled off the chair where Baldy had left them and dog-ends crowded unemptied ashtrays. A greasy frying-pan, a kettle, dirty dishes, egg-yellowed cutlery balanced precariously on the draining-board beside the sink. The table in the centre of the floor was littered with the remains of breakfast: marmalade, rolls, a milk bottle, lumpy sugar in a bowl, a brown pot of tea gone cold.

Sarah's chair was pulled as close to the fire as she could get it and still she hadn't properly thawed out. The fire blazed. Sunshine poked yellow fingers into the dingy room. She wore a woolly vest, two pairs of knickers, two woollen sweaters, ankle socks over her stockings and a scarlet scarf that covered her ears and tied under her chin but was small enough to leave most of her platinum hair sticking out.

Her blood crawled cold in her veins.

Huddled back, she closed her eyes and listened to the ticking of the clock.

If only time would stop, as she had stopped, and wait until she felt better. If only she could stay sitting here in peace and quiet, absolutely motionless, the heat of the fire mottling her legs, exhaustion suspended, senses lulled, awake, yet completely overcome as if under heavy sedation. She knew she was in her own kitchen by her own fireside and soon Baldy would come bursting through from the bedroom like a prize Aberdeen Angus bull and ravenous for his dinner. Yet she was separate, staring at the scene through black-closed lids from a place she'd floated to outside on the fringe of things. It suddenly occurred to her that this might be like dying. Immediately she opened her eyes and felt for a cigarette in her apron pocket.

She liked a smoke. Everything about the familiar habit brought comfort. The look and feel of the packet and the neat white lines of cigarettes, the promise of one rolling round between her fingers, then between her lips and sucking it before savouring the big soothing breath, then the smoke blanketing around her.

Soon she would have to heave herself up from the chair and drag herself about doing things. There was so much to be done, so many things she ought to be tackling. If she could just get organized. She strove to get sorted out in her mind, to plan her day bit by bit.

First she would set the table nice for dinner, really nice, with a nice clean table cloth. Only she hadn't got a clean cloth. All the cloths were in the lobby press with the rest of the dirty wash. The thought of mustering up enough energy to do the washing nearly swamped her.

She skipped the table.

If she washed the dishes first and put them away in the cupboard. No – put them back on the table for dinner. But there wasn't any dinner made.

If she emptied her shopping-basket first and put the things away in the cupboard, except the tin of corned beef. Baldy liked corned beef and cabbage.

The cabbage wasn't washed or chopped or cooked.

There was too much to do. She didn't know where to start. She didn't know *how* to start. She couldn't get things organized like other women – even the simplest things. She was no use. She was no use at anything.

Dragging at her cigarette, she fought to get the upper hand of her weakness.

'Aw, come on now, Sarah,' she said out loud to herself. 'Plenty folks have more tae worry them than you, hen.'

The words were barely out of her mouth when she heard the familiar thump-thump of Lender Lil at the outside door.

'But no much more!' she added wryly as she pulled herself out of the chair to go and answer it.

'About time!' her mother-in-law complained before pushing into the house.

Mrs Fowler was a big woman with a man's broad shoulders and a bosom rearing up over the top of her corsets like the Campsie Hills.

Sarah followed her back to the kitchen wondering if she would ever give up. Did Mrs Fowler really believe that she could break up their marriage and march Baldy back round to Starky Street to live forever under her thumb? Baldy wasn't daft; smiling at her mother-in-law, Sarah thought, And neither am I, you old bag!

'Like a cup of tea, hen?' she asked.

Mrs Fowler heaved her chest further up and sniffed.

'No, thanks, I'm fussy!'

Sarah shrugged. 'Suit yourself. I was just going to put the kettle on and yer welcome to a drink. Sit down and take the weight aff yer legs.'

'In a place like this? I couldn't sit in peace and I don't know how you can either. It's a disgrace. A young woman like you, too. I never kept a house like this in my life. My Baldy'll tell you. He's never been used to this.'

Sarah's face creased into a smile.

'*My* Baldy remembers how ah used to keep this place like a new pin. Ah had the floor that clean and shiny you could have ate your dinner off it.'

'I warned him. You're a fool, if you ask me, I said.

You're leaving a good clean roof over your head and three square meals a day just to go and sleep with a bastard.'

'Look, hen,' Sarah struggled to retain some modicum of good humour knowing instinctively that this was the only defence she had that Mrs Fowler didn't understand or know how to fight, 'Ah've cabbage to boil for my man's dinner. Ah haven't time to stand here listening to you calling me names. Away you go and enjoy yourself somewhere else. Away home and count your money.'

'A bastard you were. You can't deny it. I remember your ma even if you don't. A proper tart, she was, a disgrace to the street. Your granny turfed her out. Back she came, though, and you in the oven. Who your da was is anybody's guess. And your granny was nothing to boast about, either. Night and day that woman was at the bottle.' Her voice tuned up like the bagpipes. 'Night and day. If she wasn't in the pub she was in one of the shebeens. And to think my only son had to get mixed up with the likes of that.'

Distress skittered inside Sarah like panic. The kettle boiled. The lid hissed and danced. She switched off the gas, straining a cotton-wool mind to remember what else she had to do.

She lifted the heavy shopping-bag on to the table to search out the tin of corned beef and the cabbage but she had to lean her arms over the bag before looking into it, her belly pressed hard against the table's edge.

'A proper wife you cannot be to him, either,' Mrs Fowler lamented. 'How many "misses" is that you've had? I always said there was something wrong with you atween the legs. There's something wrong atween her legs, I always said.'

'There'll be something wrong between your eyes, hen, if you don't chuck it,' Sarah managed in quite a pleasant tone between grimaces.

'Strike me? Are you threatening to strike a poor old

woman, Sarah Sweeney? Of fancy! Well, go on, then. It'll be worth it to put you behind bars where you belong. I'll have the police up here to cart you away in the Black Maria before you've time to draw another breath.'

'Ah'm Sarah Fowler, *Fowler*! Now chuck it, Lil.' Eyes shimmering with pain, she felt out the cabbage, shuffled over to the sink and doubling over it, standing on one leg with the other bending and twisting in time to the spasms of abdominal pain, she cut and cleaned the cabbage and stuffed it into the pot for Baldy's dinner.

She put the gas up high and it was boiling in no time and ready long before she'd finished wandering about washing and drying the dishes, opening the tin of corned beef, frying yesterday's spuds and setting the table all to the wailings of her mother-in-law.

Nearly every day without fail Lender Lil came round from Starky Street to Dessie Street, bought her messages at MacNair's then came up to nag and criticize her and either sympathize with Baldy, splash tears over him and tell him what a poor neglected lad he was, or rage at him and cuff his ear and accuse him of being all the big fat fools of the day.

'Hello, Ma!' The reek of cabbage now filling the house brought Baldy's big square box of a body crashing into the kitchen to crush, crowd and dwarf everything, even his mother, in size. 'Hey, Sarah, that's a rer smell, hen. Cabbage, eh?'

The boom of his voice and the bang of the door as he shut it and the screech of a chair as he pulled it out and thumped down on it made Sarah wince. It was strange how noise had an effect on pain, the dragging, the bearing down labour-type pains, they jumped and strengthened with noise and flared up to catch at the breath.

'Aye, and ah've mashed it with a big dod of butter.' She grinned. 'You and your big belly.'

'You and your big bum!' Baldy thumped a hand like an

iron shovel across her buttocks, gave a coarse gravel roar of a laugh and turned to his mother again. 'How's tricks, Ma? Still coining it, eh?'

'You shut your cheeky gob!' Mrs Fowler's beady eye fought to extinguish her son's exuberance but filled with water and gave up.

Still reeling under Baldy's blow, Sarah couldn't get a grip of what was happening or where she was for a minute or two. She dished the dinner like a drunk woman.

'Could you eat some, hen?' She asked her mother-in-law automatically. 'You're welcome and there's plenty.'

'Fancy!' Mrs Fowler was genuinely exasperated. 'Dishing her man's dinner with an old pair of woolly gloves on. She's plain daft, if you ask me! A scarf round her head, too, as if the gloves weren't enough!'

'I'm awful cold rifed, amn't I, Baldy?'

'Never mind, hen, I know the way to heat you up.' With a bull-bellow he made to swipe her again but she plunked herself down at the other end of the table so quickly he missed.

She poured herself a cup of tea then wrapped her hands around it, hugged it, revelled in the heat of it. She watched Baldy enjoying his heaped high plate of food, stuffing it into his mouth with such rapidity she began to worry about his digestion.

The tea cleared her head and brought her back to grips with what was going on.

'You could have married her. You're a better man than Melvin.' Mrs Fowler sighed. 'A young thing like that, you could have trained her.'

Sarah's eyed wrinkled up with mischief.

'Hear that, Baldy. You've missed your chance, lad.'

He guffawed, squeezing a big eye shut in a muscle-hard face.

'Don't you be too sure, hen!'

Sarah sucked in another mouthful of tea.

'Today, isn't it, Lil?'

'The Band of Jesus Hall in Dundas Street. Nobody from Clydend's been invited. Just a quiet family affair Mrs Munro told Mrs Gordon. *Her* family she means, of course, but I can tell you this, everybody in this close and all old MacNair's customers are going to the Hall. Supposed to be to support Rab and Melvin but nosiness is more like it. Pity they hadn't more important things to do with their time. Anything for an excuse to dodge work and enjoy themselves, if you ask me.'

Baldy opened his mouth in a roar of laughter that made some of his cabbage spill out.

'If I know Rab he'll need supporting. He'll be as drunk as a coot.'

'Maybe I'll go!' Sarah said in between sips of tea.

'Oh, yes! Oh, of course! You've nothing else to do. Not a thing!' Mrs Fowler wiped her eyes and it occurred to Sarah that Lender Lil needed to see a doctor about this continuous overflow which surely could have nothing to do with real heartfelt tears. 'I knew it,' the older woman went on, '"I know *one*," I thought to myself, "who'll be up at that hall in Dundas Street like a flash, if you ask me!"'

Sarah crinkled with good humour.

'Ah'm no asking you, hen. I'm just going.'

She couldn't explain why she wanted to drag her weary limbs away to town to the wedding. She knew instinctively that no good would come of it.

What was that word that Jimmy Gordon once used?

A lovely fella, Jimmy. Up to the eyeballs in book-learning and it hadn't spoiled him one bit.

Massakists – that was the word!

She smiled wryly to herself.

'That's what you are, hen! You're a massakists!'

Chapter 10

Tam sat propped like a tailor's dummy between his wife Nellie and his daughter Lizzie on one of the hard wooden benches in the Band of Jesus Hall. At the other side of Lizzie perched Melvin's five-year-old son Fergus with his long blond curls like a girl and lantern jaws like an old man. Tam's whiter than white hair had been energetically brushed down and back but already the fuzzy wisps of it were springing up and spreading out in untidy excitement. His skin had been scrubbed clean and inspected by Lizzie, his shirt and collar had been starched with her usual fiendish efficiency so that he had no choice but to sit as straight and stiff as a poker with his head bulging up like a sugar-iced onion.

He felt sorry for Melvin. It looked as if Hannah Munro had won after all, because so far there wasn't a sign of the wee lassie.

He'd heard it said that Hannah was one of Christ's sergeant-majors. He chuckled to himself. He wouldn't mind being bullied by a Christian soldier like that.

Cautiously he stretched his head higher to get a better view of her sitting down front. Handsome was a better word to describe her than pretty. By God, she was a healthy looking specimen: fine ruddy cheeks, eyes full of fire, chin held high, hair thick and glossy.

Rab was a lucky man. Not content with having his fun and games with Hannah he had his bit of nonsense every now and again with Lexy as well.

Lexy would be holding the fort with Jimmy back in the bakehouse just now, bouncing and wobbling about wearing nothing but her white coat and apron. She couldn't wear anything underneath because of the heat, she always said. He could believe that. She was a hot piece of stuff was Lexy.

He wriggled restlessly in his seat, his trousers tight.

'I know what you're doing!' Lizzie hissed round at him, her pink cheeks in shadow under a wide-brimmed straw hat. 'You're annoying me on purpose. Just because I'm upset today. Everyone's trying to take advantage. Don't think I don't know. I know!'

'You're wrong, hen. Nobody's trying to get at you, honest. We're all fed up sitting here waiting so long, that's all.'

Despite his high starched collar his head twisted round in a determined effort to see something, anything, to break the monotony.

'There's Sarah! Baldy's not there, though.'

Lizzie let a titter out. 'Maybe his mammy wouldn't let him!'

Tam choked short in mid-chuckle with a wince of pain and, mouth hanging open, he eased a gentle finger round inside his collar.

'Lassie, lassie, I wish you wouldn't make things so stiff. You're choking the living daylights out of me.'

His daughter's face tightened again.

'I know how folks talk. I know their rotten twisted minds. Their tongues are busy enough flaying me and making a fool of me behind my back. They're all gloating because they've done me out of my place there beside Melvin. I know the way they've been whispering and telling lies putting him against me. They're not going to say I don't keep you clean.' Unexpectedly her elbow pierced his side. 'Look what she's wearing!'

'Who?' He wheezed in pain.

'Sarah! I'm not surprised she's cowering away at the back by herself. She ought to think shame. Look at her. What a disgrace. In church with a scarf tied round her head – a *scarlet* scarf! I wouldn't be surprised if she's wearing her slippers. Have you seen these sloppy things she wears, red and fawn check with fuzzy red stuff all round them? Supposed to be fur, all matted and greasy. She's a filthy lazy slut. Look at her. She's even too lazy to sit up straight.'

'Aw, just a minute now, hen. She never did anybody any harm. Sarah's one of the kindest souls anybody could meet. All the wee bairns in the street go daft when they see her. She's always got sweeties on her somewhere.' Tam made a brave attempt at a laugh but was given such an immediate and violent indication to remember where he was and keep quiet that he dropped his voice to an apologetic whisper.

'Och, well, she's not had much of a life. I remember when she was a bairn herself – hail, rain or shine, there she was hanging about the streets or squatting in the close or on the window-sill waiting for her granny to come home. God knows what she had to put up with when that old harridan did arrive with the key. If it hadn't been for other folk in the street giving her a bite to eat, or a cup of tea, or a wee heat at the fire, I don't think that lassie would have survived.'

'I've had to survive, and nobody helped me. They've always been jealous of me, always gossiped and whispered behind my back.'

'Don't be daft, lassie!'

His attention retreated away from her, his head tugged round in the direction of the hall door. Still no sign of the bride and her father. Rab was a queer fish. A damned good baker but close, never much chat with him. And booze? Rab could drink anybody under the table, even Baldy? Rab could be rampaging drunk one minute and that sober, that depressed the next, it would take nothing less than a bomb to break up the terrible black cloud of him.

Nellie dug into his other side.

'Here they are at last, thank goodness. If I'd had to suffer another minute on this hard seat I would have fainted. My back's just about broke.'

Rab had had a few. He wasn't staggering but he was walking so straight and stiff with his head riveted so hard back it didn't look natural.

Brother Stevens, the nervous wee budgie of a man elected to perform the ceremony, obviously didn't know whether to relax with relief at the arrival of Rab and Catriona or to keep his already twittering nerves keyed up at the ready.

'"Dearly beloved,"' he began, too soon. '"We are gathered together here in the sight of God, and in the face of this congregation, to join together this man and this woman in Holy Matrimony; which is an honourable estate . . ."'

From somewhere at the back of the hall, not at the front from the bride's family where you'd expect it, came a sniffle and the scalp-tingling beginnings of a wail.

Brother Stevens secretly cursed whoever it was.

'". . .which holy estate Christ adorned and beautified with His presence . . ."'

The sniffle became a sob.

'". . . and is commended in Holy Writ to be honourable among all men: and therefore is not by any to be taken in hand unadvisedly, lightly or wantonly; but reverently, discreetly, soberly, and in the fear of God . . ."'

Sarah's sob burst into broken-hearted words.

'Mammy, Daddy, Mammy, Daddy!'

The words swelled up to a hair-raising wail of anguish.

'Mammy, Daddy, Mammy, Daddy!'

Brother Stevens damned the woman forever in hell, *and* her mammy and daddy!

Tam nudged Lizzie then Nellie.

'What's the wee lassie trembling for? Fear of God, or Melvin, or the commotion at the back?'

Nellie sniffled a reply. 'That howling's upsetting me, Tam.'

'Not half as much as the preacher, lass. He looks as if he's going tae have a stroke.'

'Look at the disgrace of a dress!' Lizzie giggled again. 'Just look at it!'

'It was ordained for the procreation of children, for the increase of mankind according to the will of God.' Brother Stevens was so unnerved he hardly knew what he was saying. 'And that children might be brought up in the fear and nurture of the Lord . . .'

All it needed now, he thought, was for someone to stand up and object. He gazed pleadingly at the congregation.

'"If any man can show just cause why they may not lawfully be joined together, let him now declare it or forever hold his peace."'

'Mammy, Daddy, Mammy, Daddy!' howled the tear-streaked woman in the scarlet scarf, huddled in the far corner at the back.

'"I require and charge you both."' He raised his voice determined not to be beaten. '"As ye will answer at the dreadful day of judgement when the secrets of all hearts shall be disclosed, that if either of you know of any impediment, why ye may not be lawfully joined together in Matrimony, ye do confess it."'

The wailing and the sobbing reached such a pitch that everyone, including Melvin and Catriona, turned round.

Near to hysteria now, Brother Stevens shouted at Melvin's stocky back, '"Wilt thou have this Woman to thy wedded wife, to live together after God's ordinance in the holy estate of Matrimony? Wilt thou love her, comfort her, honour and keep her, in sickness and in health; and, forsaking all other, keep thee only unto her, so long as ye both shall live?"'

'Oh!' Sarah choked, exhausted at last. 'Poor, poor wee lassie!'

Chapter 11

Melvin said Lizzie would be willing to mind Fergus after the wedding for the few weeks until the Glasgow holiday fortnight started.

He didn't like leaving the business now that his father was on days instead of nights though. The days weren't so bad, especially with Jimmy on the job. It was the nights that worried Melvin. True, there was Rab and Tam and Sandy and wee Eck the halfer in the early hours, and Baldy was a good enough foreman, but they were all partial to a dram and if he wasn't there they'd be in the barm room drinking the stuff. They'd be stretched out helpless in all odd corners of the bakehouse in no time. God knows what kind of bread could be made and only Billy the horse sober enough to deliver it.

So there was no honeymoon until the Fair fortnight, and after the wedding tea they just went straight back to Dessie Street.

Melvin had decided to take the wedding night off but told Baldy that his father had instructed him to check on the bakehouse at least once during the night and they accepted this with sympathetic shaking of heads because they all knew old Duncan.

'Wipe your feet,' Melvin told Catriona as she stepped over the door holding up the long white dress she was still wearing.

She'd already wiped her feet on the prickly brown and orange mat on the landing. Now she silently repeated the process on the first little remnant of rug inside the hall. It slithered about awkwardly under her shoes on the highly polished linoleum.

'See that polish.' Melvin switched on the light and proudly surveyed the hall floor. 'Maybe you think that's a good shine. Lizzie MacGuffie thinks it's perfect and I've never bothered to contradict her but you should have seen that floor when my Betty was alive.'

'It's lovely.'

'Speak up,' Melvin rapped out. 'Nobody could hear a voice like that behind a car ticket.

'This is my bedroom.' He flung open the door with a flourish. 'I decorated it all myself.'

'It's lovely.'

'I'll put your cases down here. You can go back to your mother's and collect the rest of your things in a day or two.'

Catriona lowered her eyes.

'I haven't got any more things.'

'Eh?' He laughed and hunkered down to chug loose the strap that held the cardboard case together. 'Is this all your worldly possessions, then?'

'Please!' Spurred into action by the acuteness of her shame and embarrassment, Catriona rushed forward to tug the case away from him. 'It's my things! They're private.'

Annoyance sharpened his laughing good humour.

'You've a lot to learn about marriage, haven't you? You're young, of course, and you've never been married before. I have, you see. Betty and I had a perfect marriage. There was never any secrets between us. There's nothing private between married people, didn't you know that?'

He flicked open her case.

'An old coat, an old skirt,' he cackled, holding them up then flinging them aside. 'A jersey. A pair of knickers. A pair of flannelette pyjamas. And a hot-water bottle?'

He fell back on his buttocks slapping his knees with merriment.

'Is that all?'

Catriona snatched up the hot-water bottle and hugged it and rocked it against herself.

'Come on. I'll show you the rest of the house.' He bounced to his feet like a rubber ball. 'I bet you can't do that and you're a good few years younger than me.'

'Do what?' She stared, mystified.

'Bounce up like that without any stiff joints or breathlessness.'

He repeated the process several times, up, down, up, down, hands spread over waist, knees expanding.

'You try it!'

Clutching Lovey tighter against her chest she shook her head vigorously over the top of it, making the veil flap about.

'I shouldn't do it in my good trousers,' he admitted, leading her into the next bedroom. 'That's where Fergus sleeps. The sitting-room has big corner windows, two looking on to Dessie Street and two on to the Main Road.'

Dazedly she followed him.

'Remember,' he said, 'you saw that before. Here's the kitchen. The bathroom's there beside the front room. A nice big square hall, isn't it?'

'It's lovely.'

In the kitchen he made straight for the mirror above the mantelpiece, smoothed back his thin brown hair, tweaked out his thick waxed moustache and dusted down his trousers.

'It droops in the bakehouse, you know. The heat and the ovens.'

'What does?'

'My moustache. The wax melts. Sometimes I think I ought to shave it off but everybody says it's so manly and it suits me.'

'It's lovely.'

'What are you hugging that thing for? You look ridiculous!'

She stared down at Lovey, hugging it all the tighter.

He laughed, puffing his chest like a prize pigeon.

'You won't need any hot-water bottles when I'm around. Away through and take that awful looking dress off and get your pyjamas on while I make a cup of tea and something to eat. I'm starving.'

Gratefully she concentrated on finding her way back to the bedroom, hurrying, glad to be away from him but shuffling and tripping, held back by the too-long dress.

She banged the bedroom door and leaned against it, eyes popping, heart pattering. The thump of a man's feet shook the house, a clatter of a kettle vied with it, then the hiss of a tap turned on full.

What if he came through before she had her 'jamas' on? What if he saw her wearing nothing but her knickers?

She flung Lovey onto the bed and tore off the white dress, getting into a tangle with the thing bunched on top of her head and the sleeves too tight for her arms to escape and be rid of it. She was gasping, choking, on the verge of hysteria by the time she did disentangle herself.

A piercing whistle now, and the chinkle of cups. Shivering with panic she hopped out of her knickers and into her pyjamas.

'Come and get it!' The sudden roar from the other end of the house nearly snatched the legs from under her.

She leaned a moist quivering hand on the dressing-table.

'Come on!' The voice bawled again. 'Never mind trying to pretty yourself up. You'll do! The tea's getting cold!'

Her mind ceased to function properly. She reached for her coat and buttoned it over her pyjamas wondering how she'd transport herself back home to Fyffe Street. She couldn't be away by herself. She'd never been anywhere by herself.

Even when she'd gone to school almost directly across from the house in Fyffe Street, her mother had been by her side, escorted her back, and even waited at the gate each play-time to make her stand under a watchful eye and sip a cup of boiling hot Oxo until the bell rang.

She had always been a delicate child, her mother insisted, and not fit to play. You never knew what you might pick up from other children, bad germs, bad habits, bad things they might talk about. Anything of the male species had been especially taboo.

Her mother had kicked up a dreadful fuss at school as soon as she heard the new gym teacher was a man, and thereafter had furnished Catriona with a note that excused her from going anywhere near the gym-hall. Instead she sat in the lavatory and dreamed dreams and waited until the gym period was over.

After school there had been homework or housework, visiting with her mother, attending the meeting hall with her mother, sitting at the front-room window, or acting shops by herself.

The cupboard in the living-room beside the fire was the shop and two wooden chairs placed side by side in front of it formed the counter.

There weren't any cupboards in the kitchenette, just a shelf along the wall for dishes, so all the food was kept in the living-room cupboard.

'Yes, madam?' she'd say smartly and politely. 'Can I help you? Jam? Certainly we have jam. Which kind would madam prefer, strawberry, blackcurrant or raspberry?'

'Strawberry?' Melvin was straddling the bedroom doorway hands on his hips, moustache jerking, throat caw-cawing with laughter. 'Blackcurrant? Raspberry? She doesn't just talk to herself. She talks shop to herself. Jumpin' Jesus, I've got a right one here!'

The bed was big. A long iron bar of a bolster stretched

across it with two plumped-up pillows on top. It had grey army blankets hidden between pink flannelette sheets and a slippery rayon bedspread. The *pièce de résistance* was a thick golden cloud of satin quilt.

Catriona, blue pyjamas fastened neatly up to the neck, cringed back against the pillows, fingers digging into the pink flannelette, face closed, stiff, ashen.

'I always have my hot-water bottle!'

Unbottoning his jacket and tossing it over a chair Melvin see-sawed between hilarity and anger.

'Well, you're not having it now. This is priceless! What do you want a hot-water bottle for? It's the middle of summer as well as being your wedding night!'

'I always have my hot-water bottle!'

Watching him flick down his braces, her voice cracked and her fingers retreated under the sheets. Deftly Melvin opened his fly, stepped out of his trousers and flung them over beside his jacket.

'You're a right one, you are. Never mind, I'll soon heat you up.'

He undid his shirt then stripped it off, taking care to avoid mussing up his moustache.

'How's that for a good figure?' He admired himself in the wardrobe mirror when he was down to nothing but his underpants. 'Not bad for a man of thirty-odds?' He suddenly gripped his wrists before Catriona's horrified eyes began contorting different parts of his anatomy, making them push forward, swell grotesquely, wrench up and round while all the time he kept talking and getting a little more breathless, a little more red in the face. 'I'm not the man I used to be, of course, but I'm a miracle of fitness for a man who works nights in a bakery. Bakers are notoriously unfit. You'll never get them to admit it but they are. Stands to reason. Heart troubles, lung troubles, stomach ulcers, skin diseases, the lot. Bakers never last long. Either die or leave. We don't have them leaving so much. The houses, you see. Good houses these. My father's a crafty old devil. This building's the only one for miles around that has bathrooms. Did you know that?' He stopped talking for a minute to concentrate on doing unspeakable things to his stomach. 'See that abdominal definition?' A bulgy rolling eye demanded an answer.

Catriona slithered down in bed until only her head with a golden tangle of hair on top was showing. 'Yes,' she quavered feebly. 'It's lovely.'

'You're right,' Melvin agreed. 'Not even many champions can show an impressive "washboard" like that.'

Suddenly he began skipping with an invisible skipping rope. 'All the rest have lavies on the stairs,' he panted breathlessly. 'Most of them are just single-ends or room and kitchens and three of four families or more all share the one wee lavy. They never have lights, these lavies. You've always to take a candle or a torch.'

He stopped skipping, scratched energetically under one armpit and said:

'Ah, well! Bed!'

Immediately Catriona saw him bend, hairy hands ready to peel off his underpants, she shut her eyes.

It must be a nightmare. Her dreams had got mixed up. She twisted round on her side and curled up tight.

'"Our Father which art in heaven, hallowed be Thy name, Thy Kingdom come, Thy will be done on earth, as it is in Heaven, give us this day our daily bread and forgive us our trespasses as we forgive them that trespass against us . . ."'

Unexpectedly her whole body jarred and bounced a couple of inches up in the air as Melvin leapt into bed beside her. She kept her eyes stubbornly closed.

'"Lead us not into temptation, but deliver us from evil . . ."'

'Jumpin' Jesus,' Melvin groaned. 'Is that you talking to yourself again?'

In the tiniest most inaudible sound, more a whimper than a whisper, Catriona finished.

'"For Thine is the Kingdom, the power and the Glory, for ever and ever, Amen!"'

'Turn round then!' The bed lurched about and the blankets untucked and let draughts flap in as Melvin made himself comfortable. Catriona, a small tense ball, refused to budge a muscle.

'Come on!' With one gorilla arm he scooped her up, rolled her round and held her, nose squashed against the hairy cushion of his chest. 'Let's have a cuddle and a wee talk first. It's not often I have a night off, so enjoy it while you've got the chance.'

They lay like that for a moment before Melvin broke the silence again.

'For pity's sake, take these thick things off. They're making me sweat.'

'What things?'

'These flannelette horrors.'

Before she could wriggle an arm free to protect herself he had unbuttoned her and was tossing her from side to side and up and down until he had agitated her out of both jacket and trousers.

'That's better!' he exclaimed, one hand pinning her body to his chest. 'Now, what'll we talk about?'

Shock set in. She lay wondering vaguely if she should make some polite remark about the weather while another area of her mind convulsed and shivered like a mad thing with malaria.

'You haven't much of a chest,' Melvin remarked, holding her back a bit. 'Just like a young lady. Of course, I suppose they've time to grow yet. See mine! What a difference! There's a chest for you! A hairy chest is a sign of virility. Didn't you know that? You're lucky, you know. Not many men of my age are as well put together as me.' He flapped the blankets down again. 'Betty knew how lucky she was. She was crazy about me. Used to call me her dream man. Once when she was in hospital she wrote me some letters. I've got them in a case in that cupboard. Did you see her photo on the room mantelpiece? What did you think of it?'

'It's lovely.'

'I'll let you read the letters tomorrow.' There was a pause. Then he absent-mindedly caressed her.

'How did your wife die?'

His hand jerked clear of her.

'She was ill for a long time on and off.'

Silence.

'Fancy a cup of cocoa?' he queried eventually.

'No, thank you.'

His hand returned.

'Did your wife die having the baby?'

Again the shrinking.

'No, months after.'

It seemed he could not bring himself to touch her when he spoke of his Betty.

To Catriona this was, inexplicably, the worst, the most shameful, the most heart-rending humiliation of all.

Chapter 12

Jimmy had been too emotionally upset after reading the book even to think about playing the piano. It was a very vivid word picture of what had happened in the Highland Clearances.

A year after the defeat at the Battle of Culloden the chiefs began the terrible betrayal of their children. They decided they preferred sheep to people and drove the folk to the hills and glens from their homes with bayonets and truncheons and fire, to make way for the Lowland and English sheep-farmers.

The ill and the dying, the men, the women, the elderly folk, the young children, all with the same childish faith in the laird and all in their innocence refusing to believe the news of the burnings despite the black smoke rising high in the sky from elsewhere.

The burners came like an army – factor and fiscal, sheriff-officers, constables, shepherds, foxhunters and soldiers. They dragged out the terrified bewildered people. Families who escaped from the violence wandered aimlessly, not knowing where to find shelter or how to get their next meal.

One old man, sick with the fever, crawled into the ruins of a mill and his dog kept the rats at bay while he tried unsuccessfully to cling to life by licking flour dust from the floor. A man carried his two feverishly-ill daughters on his back for over twenty-five miles, staggering along with one, then putting her down, and going back for the other, and so on all the way.

Women watched their children die of exposure and starvation, and the tartan became a shroud.

After reading all this and more, Jimmy had locked himself in the bathroom and wept.

The trouble was, he thought, wiping his eyes with toilet paper, that people just didn't think. They didn't use their imaginations. They couldn't see events in vivid moving colour in their minds. Nobody, if they had really thought about it, really thought of what it meant in terms of human suffering, would have allowed such a monstrous thing to happen. The most important thing in the world, it seemed to him, was to try to encourage people to think, to increase their sensitivity, to develop a keen and painful edge to their imaginations.

At the height of his distress he'd tried to discuss the book with everyone but nobody wanted to listen.

His mother's normally kind, gentle voice had been impatient, almost petulant.

'It doesn't do to think so much on these things. You shouldn't read stuff like that and upset yourself and other folks. Why don't you get something nice and cheery out the library?'

Tam had still been in the bakehouse when he'd started his shift and he had actually laughed.

'Och, laddie, laddie, will you never learn to keep the head! And have a heart, son! Spare me the gory stories until I've had time to enjoy my breakfast!'

Lexy had wriggled and wobbled all over and made faces in front of him and behind his back and chanted in her sing-song Glasgow accent, 'Oh, in the name of the wee man! You're an awful big fella, so you are! Fancy getting all worked up like that about tewchters that have been pushing up the daisies for years.'

Nobody cared now as nobody cared then. All day his anguished eyes saw the suffering of the Highlanders, in the mixing-machine, in the fondant bin, in both Scotch ovens and in the proving press.

By the time he had finished a hard day's work he was

more emotionally than physically exhausted. This lack of caring, this inability or refusal to tune into other people's distress – how many more tragedies of human suffering could it lead to in the future? It seemed to him to be a most dangerous state of mind.

His mother's practised stare took rapid stock of him when he returned upstairs: the tangled curls, the dark bleak eyes, the skin tight over his cheek-bones, a peculiar putty colour.

'No sitting in here reading or playing that piano all by yourself tonight,' she told him firmly. 'You're going to the pictures or away to one of these billiard halls the other lads go to and you're going to be like them and enjoy yourself.'

'Cheeky old rascal!' Laughing, he'd pretended to spar with her. 'Trying to bully me now, are you? Put up your dukes, up your dukes, come on now, come on now!'

'Och, stop your nonsense at once and do as you're told. Away with you. Get washed and changed and get out of here.'

He had gone, to please her. But he'd hung about in the closemouth for ages watching the children playing outside in the street and wondering what he should do and where he ought to go to pass the evening.

Lanky long-legged girls hopped spring-heeled across chalked peaver beds. Others whipped draughty frames of skipping ropes round and round. Reedy voices chanted:

'Eachy-peachy, pear, plum
Out goes my chum,
My chum's not well,
Out goes mysel'.'

Boys bellowed.

'Hey, Jock, Ma Cuddy, Ma Cuddy's ower the dyke, if ye catch Ma Cuddy, ma cuddy'll gie ye a bite.'

Balls thumped monotonously.

'House to let apply within, a lady goes out for drinking gin . . .'

Everyone walking by or just clustered around enjoying the evening together grinned cheery greetings and women hanging out of windows, arms folded and leaning with breasts comfy on sills, cried out:

'Hey, Jimmy! Have you sold your piano, son?'

Or, 'Hallo there, Jimmy boy, is it the jigging the night? You're a deep one, eh? Got a wee lassie and never let on, eh?'

He hunkered down to join in a noisy game of marbles with some laughing urchins in the gutter, and was soon excitedly shouting 'Sheevies' and 'High Pots!' and 'Knucklies' with the rest of them. But his heart wasn't really in the game and after a few minutes he returned to stand at the closemouth, long thin hands gripped behind back, tall lean figure dressed in shabby but good quality Harris tweed jacket with a scarf knotted at his throat. Other people in the district bought a whole new outfit every Easter and for every Glasgow Fair. Even folks on the dole managed to get some new togs at least for the Fair, helped by the Provident and various other clubs to which they paid their shillings religiously every week (except the Fair fortnight) all through the year.

Jimmy seldom bought clothes for the simple reason that those he bought were so expensive he couldn't afford to buy them more than once every few years. He liked good things. He enjoyed the look, the line, the feel of them.

'Are you going to be next then, son?' Josy McWhirter, the painter who lived across the street, poked his face out of the window over his wife's muscle-fat shoulder. 'First old Melvin and then you. What's that wee lassie and him doing up there?' His voice heightened into a squeal of delight. 'Hey, Melvin! Can you hear me? You're awful quiet up there!'

Jimmy smiled, shook his head, raised a good-natured

fist at Josy, but felt the beginnings of a flush of embarrassment creep up from his neck. Best to make his escape before anyone noticed him actually blushing.

'Anything decent on the pictures?' he called out in what he hoped was a nonchalant manner as he strolled from the close.

Everyone immediately became intensely interested. Such a conflicting and enthusiastic bevy of film titles and criticisms assailed him and so many heated arguments arose as to whether he ought to go to the Ritzy, the local Clydend picture-house, or take the tram further afield to Govan, that he quit Dessie Street, chuckling and flapping his palms at them in mock disgust. Deciding not to bother with a tram, at least not for a few stops yet, because he felt so restless, he strode away along the Main Road towards Govan.

His pace had slowed a little by the time he was approaching Big Loui Lorretti's Ice-Cream Café, commonly known as the Tally's, which was situated at the corner of the Main Road and River Street.

He thought the crowd lounging at the corner looked familiar and, sure enough, as he got nearer he saw it was Slasher Dawson and some of the gang. Slasher was well known and feared in the district. Lil Fowler made good use of him as a muscle-man. Her extortionate rates of interest were seldom questioned when Slasher was called in to collect. Slasher had more razor scars on his face and neck that any man in Glasgow. He couldn't be much older that Jimmy but his Frankenstein stitch-puckered face and his giant humped-up shoulders made it difficult to guess his age, and nobody wanted to. Nobody wanted to do anything to Slasher Dawson or say anything about Slasher Dawson, much to many a Glasgow policeman's chagrin.

His gang in comparison were unhealthy, undersized mice, nervous fleshless ferrets as much afraid of him as anyone else but under the continual strain of trying to keep up with his crime and violence in order to please him. They had no idea of any other way to survive, living as they did around the other corner in Dixon Street where Slasher also had his abode.

Jimmy was almost alongside them before he saw Lexy. They were all around her, sniggering and chatting her up and she was laughing delightedly, patting her hair, obviously flattered at so much attention being paid to her. But he could see the winks, the leering faces, the vulgar signs behind her back and he knew what they meant.

He strolled up to the group, his heart thumping.

'Hallo, Lexy. There's a good picture on at the Lyceum. Fancy coming? You're only wasting your time hanging around here.'

For a full minute there was silence. Even Lexy was shocked rigid and could not speak.

'Say that again!' Slasher dared, still incredulous at Jimmy's audacity.

Jimmy moved nearer until his black curly head was in between Lexy and Slasher, his face almost touching Slasher's grotesque twisted nose.

'How are you doing these days, Slasher? Haven't seen you for ages.'

One of the ferrets flicked out a razor. 'Let's do him, eh? Let's carve him up!'

'Saw your sister Sadie the other day, though, and your ma!' Jimmy went on talking straight at Slasher, completely ignoring the other young man in the thin frayed suit. 'I'm making Sadie's wedding cake. I suppose you know. They were in arguing about the icing and the way the cake should be decorated. You'll be going, won't you? Going to the wedding? By the way, tell your ma I want to see her again. Tell her to come tomorrow.'

The youth brandishing the razor giggled excitedly.

'Never mind tomorrow, eh, Slasher? Come on us cover him with red icing today!'

'Shut it!' Slasher growled without looking at his minion. Then, averting his eyes from Jimmy, he shrugged. 'Aye, O.K., Jimmy. I'll tell her. Ma'll be there, don't you worry. She's goin' mad about that bloody wedding. I'm fed up hearing about it.'

Only one person in the world Slasher Dawson feared and that person was, without a doubt, his mother.

'Good!' said Jimmy. 'Well, hurry up, Lexy! I told you. It's a good picture. We won't get in if we don't get a move on!'

All at once Lexy burst into a paroxysm of hysterical giggling.

'Ohi! Ohi' she gasped and squealed. 'Oh, in the name, Jimmy Gordon. You're an awful big fella!'

Jimmy grinned and shook his head at Slasher with such obvious bonhomie that Slasher roared with laughter in return.

'Stuck with her all day and still not had enough, you big bastard.' He swung his bulk round to Lexy. 'You heard what the man said, you silly wee cow. Get movin'!'

'These heels of yours wouldn't last to the Cross,' Jimmy said. 'Come on! Here's a tram coming!'

Gripping her by the elbow he half-rushed, half carried her along the street and swung her on to the tram just as it went clanging away.

She was gasping and giggling in his arms on the tram platform when an outraged conductor burst their bubble of frivolity.

'Come oan, get aff! Naebody's allowed to canoodle on my platform!'

Pushing Lexy, but hardly able to control his own breathless laughter, Jimmy manoeuvred her into a seat. The tram was mostly filled with women wrapped in tartan shawls lumpy with dummy-sucking babies. There were only a few men in shabby suits and caps pulled well down and mufflers knotted high at their necks. Jimmy settled down beside Lexy and had just managed to subdue both his own hilarity and hers when another young woman got on at the next stop and he immediately gave up his seat to her. Strap-hanging, he swayed, lost in thought, away in another world from Lexy and tramcars until the conductor bawled: 'Govan Cross! Any of yoos for Govan Cross?'

In strange silence Lexy allowed Jimmy to assist her from the tram. Her head held high, she bristled with ice-cold dignity. Jimmy didn't notice. He had wandered back to the Highlands.

'Here, you!' Lexy erupted eventually. 'What do you think you're playing at? Who do you think you are?'

He ruffled his fingers through his hair and stared perplexedly down at her. 'I don't understand what you mean. What do you mean? What are you talking about?'

'Well, I mean to say!' Lexy patted her curls. 'A fella asks a lassie to the pictures, the next minute he's cooled off that quick he doesn't even want to sit beside her. *And you never once opened your mouth either*!' she accused with a burst of renewed anger. 'What have I ever done to you? I mean to say. I'm not infectious, you know. I suppose you'd stand in the pictures too instead of sitting beside me if you got the chance. Well, I'm *not* infectious – *see*!'

'Lexy, Lexy, love!' Jimmy was appalled. 'I didn't get up because I didn't want to sit beside you!'

Soothed by the word 'love' and the unmistakable concern on Jimmy's face, Lexy's bristles settled down, indeed began to melt away with astonishing rapidity.

He hugged an impulsive arm round her shoulders. 'It's just ordinary manners, just manners, to give up your seat to a lady in a public conveyance.'

'Och, I'm sorry, Jimmy, so I am!' She melted so close to his jacket they had some difficulty in making smooth progress into the picture house. 'I hadn't realized, I mean, you're always doing such daft things. You're an awful big fella!'

'And I was quiet because I was thinking about that book again.'

'Och, never mind, Jimmy. I mean to say. It wasn't you that done it. Och, you wouldn't hurt a fly, so you wouldn't. You just hurt yourself, so you do. Where's it to be? Back stalls, eh?' Her elbow jabbed his ribs and her squeal of laughter made him go red in the face.

He stared down, intent on finding his jacket pocket and the wallet he prayed it contained.

'Wherever you wish, of course.' He found the wallet, examined it as if he'd never set eyes on it before in his life, and selected a ten-shilling note with which to pay for the tickets.

A love film was showing inside but it paled in comparison with some of the performances taking place on the seats of the back stalls.

For Lexy's sake (after all, she was barely eighteen) Jimmy hoped she hadn't noticed as they settled in and he slithered comfortably down, long legs stretched out, elbows dug into the arms of his seat, chin resting heavily on clasped hands, ready to concentrate his full attention on the screen.

Unexpectedly, one elbow was knocked off balance, grabbed and hugged in a vice-like grip by Lexy.

'Fancy!' she hissed close to his ear. 'Just fancy! Here's me been working every day aside you and never realized you was such a lovely big fella. Ohi! Ohi! Jimmy!'

It was literally a most awkward position, terrifying, too! For a horrible minute Jimmy just sat there contorted to one side, not knowing what to do.

Then he sighed.

'Lexy. Here, sit round this way.' He put an arm around her and settled her comfortably against him.

It was her turn to sigh.

'Ohi, ohi, oh, in the name of the wee man!'

'Be quiet!' Jimmy commanded, his ears beginning to tingle with embarrassment. 'Be quiet and watch the picture. That's what we've come for, isn't it? The picture?'

'Ohi, ohi!' Lexy nearly choked. 'You're a scream, so you are. You're an awful big fella!'

Desperately he put a hand over her mouth.

'If you don't be quiet I'll make you. I'll keep my hand over your mouth like this all night!'

To his surprise she suddenly relaxed. She quietened, her head pressed against his chest, her lips moving gently against his palm. Then the hot moist tip of her tongue tickled and disturbed him.

'Lexy!'

Why, oh, why, he kept asking himself, was life so full to overflowing with worrying situations, of anxieties, of responsibilities that had to be recognized and faced up to, decisions that had to be made and acted upon?

All through the film and all the way back home to Dessie Street, despite Lexy's chatter, he thought of his responsibilities towards her.

Was he going to be just the same as people like Slasher Dawson and his mob? Did the person, the place, the background make any difference to the moral question? Did a bed instead of a back-close make it all right? Did an invitation from Lexy make it right?

Lexy was eighteen and her mother was little better than a prostitute. Lexy had moved out of her mother's house in Pelt Street to come and work as his assistant and live in one of the attic flats.

He knew she was no innocent but she was no prostitute either, though what would it matter even if she were? Was he going to give her another push along the one-way street?

No man was an island. No woman, either. If man affected man, how much more man affected woman.

A few lines from one of his favourite poets came to his mind as he took Lexy up the spiral stairs to Number 1 Dessie Street.

'Then gently scan your brother Man.
Still gentler sister Woman;
Tho' they may gang a kennin wrang,
To step aside is human
One point must still be greatly dark
The moving *why* they do it;
And just as lamely can ye mark,
How far perhaps they rue it.'

Robert Burns was a great man. An honest man and a man of wonderful love and compassion. Jimmy wondered what Burns would have thought of the Highland Clearance. He made it obvious what he thought of a national thanksgiving service being held in church for a naval victory.

'Ye hypocrites! are these your pranks?
To murder men, and gie God thanks!
For shame! gie o'er – proceed no further –
God won't accept your thanks for murder.'

Lexy rummaged in her handbag for the key to her flat. She opened the door. She smiled at him invitingly.

'Lexy!' He heaved a huge sigh. 'Oh, Lexy!'

Chapter 13

Everybody was talking about the Fair, the new clothes, the sail 'doon the watter' to Rothesay or Dunoon, the two weeks looked forward to the whole year and spent together, crowded into one comfortless room, or one room and a kitchen for which ridiculous prices were paid and paid gladly with typical Glasgow big-heartedness.

Dessie Street and surrounding district plumped for Rothesay, except Amy Gordon and Jimmy who had relations they went to visit in Dunoon. They sailed 'doon the watter' with the rest, of course. Dunoon was just not so far on. Neighbours and families crowded into the one flat, single-ends were packed, 'But and Bens', as one room and kitchens were called, were shared to overflowing, the flats next door, upstairs and downstairs were equally bursting at the seams with other neighbours for two glorious weeks.

Dessie Street, the Dessie Street side of the Main Road, Starky Street, Scotia Street, Pelt Street, Dixon Street, River Street, indeed most of Clydend, moved *en masse* to live for the Fair fortnight in even closer proximity with each other than they did for the rest of the year. And they loved every minute of it.

The only person who did not go away at the Fair was Duncan MacNair but he lived in a detached cottage in Meikle Street in the old part of Farmbank, the part that was, and he hoped always would be, unsullied by the Farmbank Corporation Housing Scheme, thanks to the huge tree-surrounded Farmbank Infirmary.

He hated the Fair (or so he said, but nobody believed him; such preposterousness was beyond any sane-minded body's understanding). All the Fair meant to him (he never tired of fighting to make them all see reason) was two weeks' loss of trade and money, a loss that would mean the ruination of him, a blow from which he would never recover.

'It'll be the death and ruination of me!' he whined through his nose to Maisie MacMahon who was filling the shelves with jars of apple jelly, and to the crowd of customers on the other side of the counter who were enjoying a blether and not paying the slightest attention to him. 'The death and ruination!'

At that point Lexy appeared from the back carrying a tray of iced German biscuits.

She was wearing her usual white coat, apron, and turban but the steel curlers were noticeably missing; instead a thick sausage curl stretched across her powdered brow, and her face was flushed under her rouge and her eyes were shining bright like torches through lashes stiff with mascara.

'Anybody for Germans? They're lovely, so they are! Jimmy's just made them!'

A howl of laughter rocked the shop and even took old Duncan by surprise.

'What the bloody hell's so funny about my German biscuits?' he snorted indignantly.

'Och, it's not your biscuits, Mr MacNair.' Tiny, gnome-like Mrs MacMahon sidled up as close to the old man as the counter would allow. 'It's Lexy. She's started going with Jimmy Gordon. Did you not know?'

Automatically Maisie MacMahon cringed back against the shelves at the sound of her mother's voice. Mrs MacMahon, tiny, humphy-backed, smiling and innocent though she might look, was still Clydend's practical joker and her family had always suffered from her jokes more than anybody else.

'She's marrying him tomorrow! It's one of them hurried

affairs.' Mrs MacMahon nodded sagely. 'You don't know what you've been missing back there. The things that go on behind that sack-cloth curtain. You wouldn't believe it.'

'No, I wouldn't, you old harridan,' Duncan MacNair replied. 'I know Jimmy. He's a cheeky bugger but he's not daft.'

'Aye, you're right, Mr MacNair,' Lexy agreed, completely unaware of the implied insult to herself.

'Och, but Lexy, hen!' Sarah squeezed to the front. 'You're no really goin' with Jimmy, are you? No harm to Jimmy. He's one of the best. A lovely fella. But ah don't think you'll get much fun out of him.' She leaned an elbow on the counter to give herself enough energy to laugh. 'Ah can't see him tickling your fancy!'

Lexy crashed the tray of German biscuits down on the counter, making old Duncan nearly weep for their fate.

'For Christ's sake!' His nasal whine loudened into a howl for help. 'Look what she's done to my Germans!'

Lexy ignored both him and his Germans and fixed a hoity-toity eye first on Sarah and then on the rest of the assembled onlookers.

'Hold your mouth, all of yoos! Jimmy Gordon's not that kind of a fella. He's cultural. And forby, he's got manners. You wouldn't get *him* sitting in front of a lady in a public convenience!'

For a minute or two everybody thought old Duncan was going to take, or had actually taken, a fit. He staggered about, bouncing first off the shelves and then off the counter, slavering at the mouth with hysterical laughter until his wispy beard was, as many a customer later described it, 'fair drookit'.

Without another word Lexy, her turbaned head held high, spun round and disappeared through the flour-sack curtain.

Gradually old Duncan was becalmed and the conversation returned to more normal channels – preparations for the Fair.

'I've heard of folk who've got some rare outfits, whole new outfits at the barras,' croaked Mrs Broderick, a comparative newcomer to the district, who had a mouth like a frog, was fat like a frog, and even had frog-like flat feet.

Suddenly the woman nearest to Mrs Broderick and to whom Mrs Broderick had so innocently spoken gave a ghastly shudder, took a menacing step that brought her even nearer to Mrs Broderick and yelled straight into Mrs Broderick's face.

'Don't you dare use that word to me. You big fat frog!' Then she stamped out the shop leaving poor Mrs Broderick blowing and puffing.

'Och, never mind, hen!' Sarah gave her a comforting pat. 'It was Mrs Tucker!' As if that explained everything.

'What did I say, but?'

'Och, nothing. It's just she can't bear the slightest thing to remind her. It all happened before your time.'

'Remind her of what, but?'

Sarah sighed. She had no inclination to use up what little store of energy she had on such ancient history but she felt sorry for Mrs Broderick who after all hadn't meant any harm, and might all too easily do the same harm again.

'Well, y'see.' She shoved back her headscarf, leaned her whole self back against the counter until she could support herself by propping her elbows on top of it, and rubbed a slippered foot up and down one leg. 'Y'see, wee Andy Tucker – that's her man – he's a stevedore, though ye wouldn't think so, he's such a delicate lookin' wee soul. I'n't he?'

She glanced around for confirmation and got it. There could be no doubt about Andy Tucker's mysterious smallness, mysterious, that was, for a stevedore who worked like a Samson in the Benlin yards. Andy was four feet nothing. He looked as if he had been chopped off at the knees and he never could get clothes, especially trousers, small enough to fit him. His trouser seats always looked like hammocks and his trouser legs were far too wide all the way down. They flapped over the edges of his shoes and became tattered at the back where he kept treading on them. If Mrs Broderick looked like a frog, wee Andy Tucker was the spitting image of a seal, flapping along the road.

'Well, anyway,' Sarah pressed on. 'You know how there's always a lot of nickin' at the yards – if it's no whisky or something like that off the boats, it's cans o' paint that's just lying around. Anyway, for a while there was an awful lot of stuff goin' a-missing. The dock-police was nearly demented. Honest, everything but the ruddy ships were being lifted and wee Andy was their chief suspect. Oh, they hud their eye on wee Andy, them police at them Benlin gates.'

'Speak up, but!' urged Mrs Broderick. 'That's an awful habit your voice has of fading away, but.'

Sarah sighed again. Then she mustered up a smile before clearing her throat.

'He kept coming out wheelin' a barra piled high and covered that careful with sacks and things. The police stopped him every time and searched under them sacks until they were even usin' magnifying glasses, no kiddin'. There was always nothing but straw, just straw, but they knew, they said, that somewhere, somehow he was hidin' whisky or even drugs or diamonds, he was sneakin' something past them somehow and they wouldn't be beat.' Her voice was fading again but she managed to end with a crinkly face and a chuckle. 'Them police nearly did their nut when they did find oot what Andy was nickin'.'

'What, but?'

'The ruddy barras!'

Mrs Broderick opened an enormous mouth and let go such a yell of laughter she nearly burst her stays.

'Oh, what a scream, but!' She flapped, web-footed, towards the door, hitching herself together as best she could. 'Oh, here, I'd better away if I've tae be ready for the Fair tomorrow. I'll never reach the Broomilaw at this rate, but.'

Sarah's chest lifted with another big sigh. Sigh, sigh, sigh – it was all she could do these days. Still, a couple of weeks at Rothesay would soon put her right.

'Ah'm away as well.' She hoisted her basket over her arm. 'Ah haven't a thing done. No even a case packed.'

But she'd manage somehow, she knew. Anything to get away for a change, a paddle in the water, a breath of fresh air, anything to make her feel better.

She took a long time dragging herself up the stairs and felt most peculiar when she reached her own door on the second landing. A singing noise made light of her head and her tongue felt thick and tingly.

'Baldy!'

She felt her way into the silent house.

'Baldy!'

She shivered. 'Aw, come on, hen!' she begged herself. 'You've your man's tea to make and you've your case to pack. Just think of the morra. The morra, hen! That lovely sail doon the watter. And Rothesay! Aw, come on, hen. If you can just get yersel there, you're all right. You're a lucky lassie now. Come on. Come on. Count your blessings. At least your man's a foreman and he's got the money. All you need is the strength!'

The words were barely out of her mouth when the doorbell startled her. She wasn't expecting anybody except Baldy and of course it wouldn't be him because he had a key. She shuffled to the door using the wall to support her, trying all the time to gather enough energy to make herself smile and be ready to talk pleasantly.

It *was* Baldy, although he was barely recognizable. A taxi-driver was holding him up.

Sarah swallowed down her sickness.

'What happened?'

'Don't worry, hen!' Baldy swayed, bloody-faced, towards her, chunks of flesh sticking out and beginning to turn black. 'Ah'm perfi-per-per . . . Ah'm O.K. Ah just had a couple too many and tripped over masel'.' All at once he exploded into riotous song. 'I belong tae Glasgow! Dear old Glasgow town!'

The taxi-driver groaned.

'For pity's sake, man. Look at your nice wee wife. What makes you do a thing like this? Why do you live like this?'

Baldy pushed him aside and lurched into the house to tower over both Sarah and the cab-driver.

'Och, you silly wee ninny. If you haven't buried your face in the concrete you're not a man and you haven't lived!' Then his face squeezed into a smile and bled down at Sarah.

'Ah, there's my wee wifie waitin'. Pay the man, hen. I'm skint.' Suddenly he became very, very polite. 'I have not one halfpenny left in my possession.'

And with that he wended a zig-zag, hiccoughing, merry path towards the sink in the kitchen.

Chapter 14

The knock on the door was very quiet, so quiet that Catriona went on polishing the sitting-room surround, hearing it, yet not hearing anything at all.

Betty, Melvin's first wife, was a marvellous woman. Her death-bed had been the settee, under which Catriona was now sweating. It had been drawn close to the window so that Betty could be propped up to gaze down at life milling past in Dessie Street.

Melvin had done the housework during the day as well as work in the bakehouse at night and in the last few months of Betty's life he had looked after baby Fergus as well.

Betty adored him, he said, and couldn't bear that he should only be able to take a few hours' sleep and then have to get up to scrub and polish. Melvin liked the carpets scrubbed but everything else in the house protected by a hard gleaming polish. Many a time, he said, he found Betty creeping round the sitting-room floor in her nightie with a duster in her hand trying to save him the bother of doing the polishing.

Catriona wriggled from under the settee and squatted breathlessly back on her hunkers to gaze up at the huge golden-framed photograph of Betty that dominated the sitting-room mantelpiece. There was a medium-sized photo in the kitchen and one in the bedroom as well.

The knock at the door did not become louder but it quickened with irritation and insistence.

Catriona struggled to her feet and hurried out to the hall to open it.

A woman and a child of about five stood on the doormat. The woman had straight hair, a pink and white complexion and eyes like splinters of coal.

'I didn't knock loud,' she whispered, 'in case Melvin would be sleeping.'

'Won't you come in, please. You must be Lizzie.'

The child clung to Lizzie's hand. 'Want to stay with you.'

'I know you do, my wee son. You know who's good to you, don't you? Who gives you sweeties, eh?'

Catriona began to feel uneasy but she stifled her qualms and asked Lizzie to stay for a cup of tea.

'Sweetened with arsenic, I suppose,' Lizzie replied.

'What do you mean?'

'You can't fool me. I know you've had it in for me right from the start.'

'I never even heard of you until the other day. Why should I want to do you any harm? I just want to be friends with everybody.'

Catriona shot the pale-faced little boy a worried glance. How did one talk to a child?

'Hallo.' Reaching the sitting-room she riveted her attention on him. 'You must be Fergus. I'm . . . I'm . . . You saw me at the Hall, didn't you? But your Aunty Lizzie took you home early so I didn't see you.'

'Don't you dare! I'm warning you. I'll see through every one of your tricks.'

'What tricks? What are you talking about now?'

'Trying to put my wee Fergie, my wee precious boy, against me. Me who's loved and cared for him like a mother!'

Catriona's heart thumped.

'I said you took him away from the Hall early. I was telling no lie or playing no trick. You *did* take him away early but no doubt you did the right thing. Little children have to go to bed early, haven't they?'

'I've been like a mother to that child and better. The

fun we've had!' She smiled at him, bending over. 'Eh, Fergie?'

'I was hoping you'd help me.'

The child, who'd been like a wax dummy, suddenly exploded. 'I want my toys! I want my toys! I want my toys!' Leaping up and down, he zig-zagged in a mad dance around the room.

Catriona gaped at him.

'He's Aunty Lizzie's wee precious son.' Lizzie's voice dropped to a whisper. 'Aunty Lizzie will never be far away. Aunty Lizzie will always be waiting, across the landing, waiting behind her door.'

'Just a minute!' By the time Catriona recovered, Lizzie had limped heavily away.

'I wanted to talk to you,' she called after her.

The front door quietly shut.

'I want my toys! I want my toys! I want my toys!'

The mad dance erupted into the hall.

'Hush! Fergus! For pity's sake. You'll waken Daddy. Be quiet!' She chased after the tiny savage into his bedroom and immediately let out a cry of pain as a well-aimed metal toy hurtled through the air, and hit her in the chest.

Her mouth opened. Her face contorted. In agony she nursed her breast.

Other toys pelted about. Her nostrils widened as she fought for breath. Something sharp stung her leg.

'Stop it! Stop it at once!'

With arms outstretched she stumbled blindly towards him. Her hands found his dark-green jersey. She felt like stran- gling him but at the same time horror at herself changed her voice, pushed it back down her throat, gentled it.

'I'm your new mummy.'

He stopped. He stared warily up at her.

Her unexpected surge of passion evaporated as quickly

as it had fumed into life and she gazed at the little boy with nothing but innocent curiosity.

He seemed to have calmed, too; a wax dummy again, his eyes a bright still blue.

She smiled.

'We're going to be friends, aren't we?' Her mind roamed dreamily, searching for nice things to say. 'We're going to live together in this lovely house forever and ever and I'm going to love you and look after you like a real mummy and we're going to be happy and safe here together for always.'

How still he was! She'd never seen anyone or anything so motionless. Time stopped, life gone, only caution clung round his small bird-like figure, his long girlish curls. Then, with astounding rapidity, he lunged at her, his nails digging deep into her legs.

'Fergus, what are you doing?' She endeavoured, gently at first, to pull him off. 'You're hurting me!'

He was hugging her legs with the strength of an iron-muscled maniac, his face hidden hard in her skirts.

'Fergus, don't be silly, dear.' Wrenching at him with increasing vigour but without the slightest success she fought to free herself. 'Fergus!' Her voice condensed in a flurry of alarm as her soft fingers, poking and prising at his fingers, found them statue hard, unbendable.

She didn't know what to do. She was a child herself, terrified.

'Melvin! Melvin! Melvin!'

The silky head moved. Fergus looked up at her, and in the moment before he released her, she saw the gleam of perverted delight in his eyes.

By the time Melvin had staggered through from the next bedroom in answer to her screams, unshaven, moustache mussed, face pouchy with sleep, hands fumbling with the cord of his dressing-gown, his son was quietly tidying away toys.

'Hello, Daddy!'

'Hallo, son.' A mumble before turning to Catriona and coarsening his voice. 'What were you making all that racket for? You wakened me out of a good sleep.'

Catriona stared at Fergus. She wondered if she'd imagined the whole thing.

'I'm sorry.' Her eyes flickered round to Melvin then lowered in embarrassment. 'It . . . it . . . it was nothing. I . . . mean . . . I . . . I . . . think.'

'Stop stuttering!' She caught the note of disgust and flinched under it. 'You sound like an idiot. And keep your eyes up when people talk to you. You look like a terrified mouse. We're not going to eat her, are we, Fergus?'

Unexpectedly he laughed, flung an arm round her shoulders, and kissed her wetly, searchingly and for too long on the mouth.

The child's eyes were burning a hole in her back.

In desperation she wriggled free. Melvin laughed again.

'Just kiss her.' He wiped his mouth with the back of his hand. 'Eh, Fergus?'

'Not in front of the child.'

'Why not?'

She didn't know why not.

'Why not?' Melvin repeated.

'I don't think he likes you kissing me.'

'Don't be daft. Why shouldn't he like anything I do? He's my boy. I brought him up myself. He's the best behaved child in Scotland. Lizzie likes to think she's helped and I let her think it to keep her happy but I looked after my son from the moment he was born. You like Daddy to kiss your new mummy, don't you, Fergus?'

Fergus nodded.

'See!' Melvin nudged Catriona. 'What did I tell you? You're daft! Come on through to the kitchen.' In the hall his tone turned conspiratorial. 'I'll show you how well-behaved and well-disciplined my boy is. Just wait till you see this. Fergus!' he called heartily as soon as he reached the kitchen. 'Come through here, son. Come and see what Daddy's got!'

By the time the child had arrived to stand before him, Melvin had produced two bags of sweets from the cabinet drawer.

'A bag of sweeties for Mummy.' He handed Catriona one of the paper bags. 'And a bag of sweeties for Daddy.'

A silence followed.

Catriona stood uncomprehendingly.

Melvin popped a toffee ball into his mouth and began sucking.

'Mm . . . good! Come on!' His eyes bulged impatiently first at her and then at the bag in her hand. 'You put one in your mouth, stupid! Hurry up!'

Well-trained to jump automatically to sharp command, she pushed a sweet into her mouth.

She felt sick.

'There now!' Melvin sighed with satisfaction. 'And what have you been doing today, son? Been having a good time, have you?'

'Yes, thank you, Daddy.'

'Right, away back and play with your toys, then.'

Fergus turned and walked obediently away.

'See that!' Melvin chewed the toffee ball over to the other side of his unshaven face. 'What did you think of that, eh?'

Catriona removed the sweet from her own mouth as delicately as possible. A twitch fluttered like a butterfly at her temple.

'I thought it was horrible.'

'Not the sweet, you fool,' Melvin laughed. 'Fergus! Anyway there's nothing wrong with the toffee balls. The old man sells them in the shop. There's very little he doesn't sell. Everything from a pan loaf to a sanitary towel. Well?'

She felt frightened. She didn't understand his lack of understanding.

'You tormented the child. It was horrible!'

'Don't be stupid. Fergus knows he can get sweets any day of the week. He can get anything he fancies out of the shop and I'm always buying him things up the town. See all these toys through there. I bought these for my son. There isn't another child in Glasgow who's got toys like some of those through there. Did you not see the size of that rocking-horse? And I always buy him a present for going away with at the Fair. Do you know what I've got for him this year? It's still down at the bakehouse. I was showing it to the men. What a laugh we had with it. It's a toy monkey. A big stuffed thing and real-life-size. I'll go down and get it later on.'

'Maybe you didn't mean to, but . . .'

'But what? My son's obedient and well-trained, that's what! Have you ever seen a child who could walk quietly away like that after everybody's got sweets but him? Have you ever seen a child like that before?'

'No, but . . .'

'Did he stamp his feet? Did he go into a temper? Did he shout and bawl: "I want sweeties. I want sweeties"?'

'No, but, Melvin . . .'

'Did my son cry?'

'He should have!' Catriona's voice teetered unexpectedly out of control. 'He should have cried and cried. A child should cry when he gets hurt.'

'Och, shut up. Don't talk daft. Obviously you've a lot to learn about me. Anybody in Clydend could tell you how devoted I've been to that boy. Hurt him? Me? You're a fool. More like you hurting him. What were you doing to him when I came through just now? Fighting with him, were you? Was that what all the screaming and fuss was about? I bet you cried when you were a child, always snivelling, I bet.'

Only now did it enter her head that she had never cried when she was a child.

'Where has his crying gone?' she insisted.

'Eh?' Melvin flung back his head and roared with laughter. 'That's priceless, that is! Where has his crying gone? Sounds like a line from a song.' Suddenly he blustered into the old Scottish tune 'Wha saw the Tattie Hawkers?' and went clopping round the kitchen like a Clydesdale carthorse. 'Where has his crying gone – where has his crying gone – where has his crying gone – it's gone up the Broomilaw!'

Catriona's mind retreated back to the bedroom to Fergus.

'Come on!' Melvin grabbed her, jigged her around a couple of times before stopping to fondle her. 'Remember we're off for our holidays tomorrow.'

Her eyes strained nervously towards the door.

'What's wrong?' Melvin pressed himself against her. 'What are you looking so frightened for?'

Catriona bunched her fists against his chest.

'The child might come in.'

'So what?' He pushed forward until he had made her stagger and fall into the cushions of the fireside chair. He lay heavy on top of her. 'My dressing-gown's tucked around you. He won't see anything.'

Shivering violently, pinned down by the weight of Melvin, her mind darted about seeking some solid ground of understanding, some yardstick by which she could properly measure the rightness or wrongness of events.

Betty's letters had been loving to the point of painful embarrassment. It had been an agony to read them. Never before in her life had she been so acutely distressed. 'My dream man' and 'my wonderful passionate lover' were favourite phrases of Betty's.

From the cheap notepaper and the weak spidery scrawl had emerged the unmistakable and almost grovelling gratitude of a young girl already condemned to death but clinging desperately to the image of herself as a loving and vital woman – 'Any day now I'll be able to return to you and lie beside you and be a *real* wife to you, the kind of wife you want.' 'Please forgive me for being ill' was another phrase which kept recurring with harrowing insistency. 'Please be patient with me. Soon I'll be lying at your side and I'll be able to turn to you and love you and love you with all the energy that's in me. I'll be everything a good wife should. Everything and more, much more. Melvin, Melvin, I promise you, if you'll only love me still, and be patient.'

'If you're half as good a wife as Betty,' Melvin had informed her as he had pushed yet another letter under her nose, 'you'll do all right. You've a lot to learn though, but don't worry too much about it. I'll teach you just as I taught her.'

Now, over Melvin's shoulder she saw the kitchen door open and Fergus appear.

'The child!' she cried breathlessly. 'The child!'

'Aw, shut up!' Melvin breathed hoarsely in her ear.

Fergus had eyes like blue diamonds.

'Oh, Melvin . . . Oh, Melvin, please!'

The knocking at the outside door came straight from God, straight from the good Lord, to save her.

'Melvin, somebody's at the door.'

'Who the Hell can that be?' He heaved himself up, furious, hardly giving her time to twist round and hide herself from the diamond eyes and rearrange her clothing.

'Well, go on!' he fumed. 'Answer it.'

Hardly aware of what she was doing or where she was going, Catriona ran pell-mell into the hall and jerked open the door.

'Yes?'

For a minute Amy Gordon lost her voice. She stared at the pale sweating face, the expanding nostrils, the huge amber eyes filled to overflowing with what looked like terror.

'I'm Mrs Gordon from upstairs, remember?' Her freckled motherly face softened into a puzzled, question-smile. 'Are you feeling all right, dear?'

Catriona longed to throw herself into the old woman's arms and beg for help and protection but a lifetime of training in the virtues of self-discipline and an inborn Scottish embarrassment at melodramatic displays of emotion kept her firmly in check.

She lowered eyes and voice. 'Yes, thank you.'

'I brought you some of my home-baked scones and I wondered if you needed a hand with your packing. You'll hardly have had time to settle in Dessie Street, never mind get ready to go away to Rothesay.'

'Please come in!' Catriona led the way to the front room. 'It's awfully kind of you. The scones look delicious. Thank you very much. Can I make you a cup of tea or something?'

Mrs Gordon arranged her plump body comfortably on the settee by the window. 'Well, I really came to help you not to hinder you, dear,' she laughed. 'But I never say no to a nice cup of tea.'

'Oh, thank you. You're so kind. I won't be a minute.' Catriona backed stumbling towards the door, clutching the plate of scones against herself as if she were terrified they'd take wings and fly away. 'I'll just run through to the kitchen and put the kettle on. I won't be a minute. Please don't go away.'

She left Mrs Gordon more perplexed than ever, but amused too; shaking her head and chuckling.

Melvin was tucking his shirt into his trousers in front of the kitchen fire. He always liked to get dressed in front of a fire.

'What the hell does she want?' His whisper rasped like sandpaper.

'To help me.' Flushed with excitement Catriona splashed water into the kettle and lit the gas cooker.

'Well, tell her you don't need any help! You've got me!'

She flung a curious glance at him as she clattered cups and saucers on to a tray. It seemed very odd to whisper when the whole width of the hall and more was between them and Mrs Gordon – and both the front room and the kitchen doors were shut.

'But the packing and everything. Women's kind of work.'

'I can do anything a woman can do and better. Cooking and baking's supposed to be a woman's job but I've yet to meet the woman who could cook a better meal or bake a better loaf than me!' He growled at her. 'You're not going to have females filling my house from morning till night. Tell her the packing's done and get rid of her.'

'But I've promised her a cup of tea. She's through in the front room waiting. And she brought scones – see, aren't they lovely? Wasn't that kind?'

'Stop your idiotic chattering! I've got a bakehouse of scones downstairs. Give her the tea and get rid of her as quick as you can. I want to talk to you. I can see I'll have to talk to you. There's a lot you don't know about marriage. And anyway,' his whisper strained as loud as his throat would allow, 'I've enough to suffer with Jimmy's piano. Sometimes I can't even hear the boxing. He drowns out my wireless. He's worse than the blasted riveters over at Benlin's.'

'What?' Her head was reeling as she rushed around making the tea and finding a milk jug and sugar bowl. 'Who's Jimmy?'

'Her son. Oh, you'll soon find out all about Jimmy. She never stops talking about him. A tall curly-haired bloke. You must have seen him at the Govan Fair. He was tossing pancakes on the float. He works days. He's our confectioner. Look what you're doing! You've spilt milk on my good tray. That'll seep under the glass now.'

'I'm sorry.'

She hurried for a cloth but he beat her to it and reverently mopped up the milk. 'I made that tray.'

'It's lovely.'

'Carry it carefully and watch my good dishes, and remember I've done the packing and I want to talk to you.'

The tray sped across the hall, milk leaping, splashing, dishes, spoons clattering, chinkling, hysterical.

'Saints alive!' Mrs Gordon laughed out loud when Catriona exploded into the room. 'You're an awful wee lassie. But never mind, you'll soon settle down.' She accepted an eagerly proffered cup of tea with a sigh of pleasure. 'I understood your mother being upset, of course, with everything being so unexpected, and Melvin being a good bit older than you, but your mother doesn't really know Melvin or any of us very well, does she? No, thank you, I won't have a scone, dear; but you eat them up. You're such a skinny wee thing. I know who your mother was, of course. God forgive me, I don't manage to Meeting very often but I have heard her speak. A wonderful woman. You must be very proud of her. And I'm sure everything will work out all right and you'll be able to tell her not to worry. Are you listening to me, dear?'

'I'm sorry. What did you say?'

'Melvin MacNair is a good man.'

'Oh?' Amber eyes grew large, desperate to learn, yet astonished. 'Is he?'

Chapter 15

Sandy had been so upset when he'd heard about Baldy drinking and gambling away all his holiday money, he'd taken twice as long as normal to clear out his van.

His tall telegraph-pole figure, topped by his padded cap and the bread-boards, drooped in and out the Dessie Street close, tender feet pecking the ground like a hen on tiptoe.

He was thinking about Sarah, not Baldy. 'Poor wee thing.' He puffed and puttered into the bakehouse. 'And her looking as if she could be doing with a holiday, too!'

Jimmy shook his head, his young face a picture of misery, so keenly was he feeling Sarah's plight.

'How could Baldy do it? What harm has Sarah done anybody? What harm?'

Tam lifted his checked cloth cap to give his head a good scratch. He had escaped back down to the bakehouse as fast as he could. He was always escaping somewhere, the street corner, the pub, the bookie's, anywhere away from his own home and family. 'We'll have to all pitch in. We'll have to do something.'

Sandy's bloodhound mouth pulled down.

'Aye, but what?'

'Put round the hat, you mean?' Jimmy stopped piping cream into the sponges and looked up, eyes on fire. 'Start a collection?'

'Aye, son!' Tam smacked and rubbed his hands together. 'The very thing!'

Sandy's lip jerked out and in for a minute.

'There's not much time, Tam, and folks haven't much money to spare these days.'

‘Och, don’t fash yourself, Sanny. You know folks’ll give as much as they can. I’ll do the organizing. I’ll go round everybody in the close for a start. Then the street. Even if everybody gives just a few coppers it’ll be enough.’

‘I could take you round the rest of the streets in the van.’

‘Good man!’

‘And we could trot over to Farmbank. Rab would want to give something. That’s one thing about Rab. He’s not mean. Nor’s that wife of his. She’d give you the shirt off her back I’ve heard.’

‘Christ, that’s something I’d like to see – the shirt off her back!’

Sandy’s teeth and gums came into view but Jimmy cut hilarity short.

‘Tam, keep to the point. It’s true what Sandy says. There isn’t much time and everybody’s busy getting ready for tomorrow.’

‘Aye, you’re right, Jimmy.’ Sandy sobered down, then suddenly leapt into unexpected and unusual life. ‘That bloody cuddy!’ he yelled, and rushed away in an agony of speed as if he were propelling himself through a minefield.

He was too late! Billy the horse had heard the Benlin hooter and was off like Tam O’Shanter’s mare, hell-bent for home.

Billy knew, the same as anybody else, and by the same token, that knocking off time was time to knock off.

‘Ya bloody cuddy!’ Sandy shook a furious fist at the horse and dangerously rocking, rollicking van as they disappeared into the distance, away along the Main Road. ‘I’ll get you for this. I’ll teach you yet you stupid old ass!’

He drooped slowly back to the bakehouse where both Lexy and wee Eck were hugging each other, holding each other up, staggering about bumping into things, hysterical with laughter.

He puttered gloomily at them.

‘I’ll fillet that beast yet. I’ll break every bone in his body.’

Not even Jimmy was shocked by this remark. It was common knowledge that Sandy McNulty loved Billy the horse, and often talked to the animal like a brother.

‘Och, keep the head, Sanny. Take the tram along to the stables if your feet can’t thole the walking.’

‘One of them days, Tam, that bloody cuddy will do that once too often to me.’

‘Well, then.’ Tam hitched up his shoulders, smacked and rubbed his hands together. ‘That’s it settled, eh? We all put in as much as we can and get everybody else to do the same.’

‘Great, Tam!’ Jimmy radiated enthusiasm. ‘Just great!’

‘I’m away up, then.’ Tam gave the vanman his usual punch as he passed, making Sandy’s sad eyes roll and his red nose redden. ‘You go and fetch King Billy while I pass the hat round the close.’

Melvin straddled the front of the fire, thumbs hooked in braces.

‘Marriage,’ he announced, ‘is like two raindrops trickling down a window-pane, running into one another and becoming one.’

A giggle sprang unexpectedly to Catriona’s lips, horrifying both Melvin and herself.

An outraged eye bulged down at her.

‘I have always believed that marriage was a serious business. You obviously think it’s just a joke.’

‘Oh, no!’ she hastened to assure him. ‘Oh, no, I don’t.’

‘Well, what are you snickering for?’

She lowered her eyes.

‘I’m sorry, Melvin. I don’t know what made me do it. What were you saying?’

He fondled his moustache, hesitated, then once more took the plunge.

‘Marriage is like two raindrops trickling down a window-pane, running into one another and becoming one.’

Sitting on the fireside chair, hands clasped demurely on lap, Catriona kept her head bent low.

'You're doing it again!' he accused.

'Maybe it's the idea of you being a raindrop. I mean . . . I mean . . . Oh, Melvin, please let me laugh!'

He didn't reply but a sound rumbled up from his chest like far-off thunder until it exploded in an open-mouthed roar of hilarity.

She smacked her hands over her mouth as if afraid she would go completely berserk.

Soon they were both mopping up tears of mirth that had all but exhausted them.

'OK! OK!' Melvin was first to recover. 'So I'm no raindrop. So shut up and listen to what I've got to tell you. Get up and let me sit there. Here, sit on my knee and sit quiet and serious and behave yourself.'

Not many occasions in her life had been happy ones. But she felt happy now. Sitting on Melvin's knee, her head held back against his shoulder, she remembered years ago being held like this by her father. The house had been very still and empty. They had clung together in silence and she had felt safe.

Melvin was restless.

'I mean this!' He cleared his throat. 'I'm not like most Scotsmen. The men round about here, for instance, make me sick. To them a wife's just part of their goods and chattels and their homes are just hotel rooms or lodging houses, places where they sleep and eat and get dressed to go out to football matches or pubs or bookies or out somewhere with the lads. Not me, I'm all for my home, and my wife and family. I've no interest at all outside this house unless it's to take my wife and family somewhere. And I neither gamble nor drink. I don't believe in wasting good money. That's why I always have a shilling or two in my pocket and a pound or two in the bank. Are you listening to me? It's time you gave yourself a shake and woke yourself up. There's always such a faraway dreamy look about you.'

'No, I'm listening, Melvin!'

'Well, anyway, as I said, I believe a happy marriage should be two people like one but living for each other, doing things for each other, trying to make each other happy all the time. To be a good wife you ought to study my every wish and comfort and your whole life from now on should be wrapped up in that. And I'll do everything humanly possible to see that you lack absolutely nothing to make you happy and keep you satisfied.' He suddenly gurgled. 'I keep you sexually satisfied, don't I? I know my sex, eh?'

This could not be denied so she kept silent. He turned serious too.

'There's something wrong with a marriage, I always say, if it needs to depend on anything from outsiders.'

Her eyes stretched with surprise. 'From outsiders?'

'Take Mrs Gordon, for instance. She was in here like a flash. She thinks it's going to be different because it's a different wife. Well, it's not. It's a wonder Sarah hasn't been. She's usually first.'

Catriona shook her head.

'You jump about from one thing to another. I can't keep up with you.'

'Yes,' he agreed, giving her an affectionate pat. 'I've a quick mind and you're pathetically slow. Never mind, I'll soon get you trained.'

'But I get mixed up with them all. Who's Sarah?'

'Baldy Fowler's wife. The silly fool that spoiled our wedding day.'

'Oh, dear, wasn't it awful?'

'She's an idiot and a dirty slut into the bargain. You could stir that woman's house with a stick. But never mind her. The point is they would all be in and out here like yo-yos if you let them. That's the way they live. It would fit them better to mind their own business and keep themselves to themselves and busy themselves cleaning their houses.'

He tidied his moustache, smoothed, twirled it, pushed it up at the edges. 'But never mind any of them! The point is, we don't need anybody if we're happily married. There's something wrong with a marriage, I always say, if the couple can't satisfy each other's every need.' His gaze acquired a hint of reprimand. 'Betty and I were perfectly happy together.'

Catriona sighed.

'What are you sighing for? What have you got to sigh about? You've a good husband, a ready-made child and a lovely home. What more could a woman want?'

'I was just thinking that I'll never be able to be as good a wife as Betty. She seems to have had everything, even looks.'

'Oh, you'll do – if you do as you're told. I mean – if you just concentrate on your husband, your home and your family, that's all I'm saying. A good marriage doesn't need neighbours or friends or relations or anybody. Betty was an orphan.'

'Poor thing!'

'What's poor about that? You're better without parents half the time. All they do is interfere and try and cause trouble. Betty didn't need anybody. She had me! She dropped her girl friends, even her best friend after we got married. Never saw them again, until the night before she died. I knew she couldn't last another night – down to skin and bone Betty was – a terrible sight. So I thought I'd give her a wee treat. She had been awful fond of that best friend – Jenny – Jenny something her name was. Funny how you forget. I've forgotten it now. Anyway I thought my Betty would like to see Jenny before she died so I sent for her and she came and I let her stay the night. Betty died the next morning. We were both with her – Jenny and I.'

A long silence followed in which Melvin played with his moustache and his eyes became glazed, remembering.

Catriona's mind darted about in distress. She looked round at the photo of Betty on the kitchen mantelpiece, stared perplexedly at the sad still eyes.

'Melvin, are you sure you're right? It says in the Bible to love thy neighbour.'

'Obviously Jesus Christ never knew Dessie Street or Starky Street or any of the streets around here or He'd never have said a daft thing like that.'

'But when Peter asked Jesus how often he was supposed to forgive people who'd sinned against him – "As many as seven times?" he asked, and Jesus said, "I do not say to you seven times, but seventy times seven."'

'Aw, shut up! You sound just like your mother!' He jerked her roughly off his knee and away from him. 'And I'm having neither your mother nor anybody like her in here. She knows her Bible, doesn't she? But a lot of good her knowing it did you! A squashed, dominated, stuttering little nonentity, that's what her and her holiness did to you. Folk like your mother are the biggest and worst kind of hypocrites in the world and they ought to be shot! They just use their religion to frighten folk and to get their own way. I bet your mother's frightened you silly all your life, eh? Hasn't she?'

Too many memories of too many fear-filled days and nights, of visions of retributions known and unknown clawed over Catriona's nerves. They could not be denied.

She stood before Melvin, head bent low, fingers twisting, a contrite child made all the more wretched by his withdrawal of affection.

'I'm sorry, Melvin.'

'I don't want your hypocrites in here.'

'I'm sorry.'

'You're young. You've a lot to learn about life and people.'

'I know.'

'That's what makes me laugh about you.' Unexpectedly he let out a guffaw. 'You always agree with everything anybody says about you. Good God!' His expression changed. 'That's that door again. Watch out of my way! This time *I'll* go!'

She remained facing his empty chair, her mind suspended with surprise. It had never occurred to her to disagree with anyone's criticism of herself. The mere idea was both astonishing and intriguing. And she had Melvin to thank for planting the idea in her head.

'Come away through, Tam.' Melvin returned, and gave his eyes a rapid roll towards the ceiling before turning to reveal the little white-haired swagger of a man behind him.

'Hallo, there!' Tam tossed his cap from his right hand to his left and came sauntering bouncily towards her, right hand outstretched.

'I'm Tam MacGuffie, your next-door neighbour, hen! Welcome to Dessie Street. You're a bonny wee lassie.' He grabbed her hand and pumped it up and down with such fervour she marvelled at the strength of him. 'We'll be seeing you at Rothesay, eh?'

'Not if we see you first!' said Melvin. 'Here's a quid and tell Baldy from me, he'd better watch it. I'll have his guts for garters one of these days!'

Catriona flushed a bright scarlet, tried to smile but failed and struggled to find enough voice to apologize for Melvin.

'Aye, he's a lad, is Baldy.' Tam laughed, apparently not in the least offended. 'Thanks, Melvin. You're a good sport, so you are.' He punched Catriona's arm and she staggered sideways against the chair and sat down with a thump. 'You're a lucky wee lassie to have a man like this. I hope you realize that.'

He squared up to Melvin as he passed him, ducked a

couple of times then landed a good-natured punch on Melvin's chest before trotting out of the kitchen. 'I've to meet Sanny. He's away along the Main Road chasing after his horse. Cheerio the now, hen,' he shouted from the hall. 'I hope you enjoy your sail doon the watter tomorrow! We'll all be there all together. Och, it's grand, so it is. You'll love it.'

Chapter 16

Rab had felt depressed before but never so hopelessly as he felt now. Looking back on his life he saw it as a complete waste of time and he blamed nobody but himself for his failures.

Low in his chair, head sunk forward, shaggy brows down, clothes hanging loose over big bones, he ignored Hannah's tirade, allowed it to pass him by, but in doing so each low-pitched, husky, nagging word sucked more of his vitality from him.

He did not need to argue with Hannah or answer her back or even listen to her to exhaust himself.

He recognized the fact, of course, that he never got enough sleep. Hannah's friends and neighbours were forever banging in and out of the house while he tossed and turned in the bedroom and punched his pillows and fervently wished eternal damnation on every member of the Band of Jesus.

Nevertheless the responsibility remained with him. It was his house and his wife and he ought to be able to keep both to his liking.

He had tried. Oh, he had tried, all right. He had accepted the challenge, fought the good fight – and been beaten. He'd tried to escape and been successful for a wee while but now even Lexy had grown sick of him.

She had asked for the return of her key. No explanation, no tender goodbyes, no regrets, no nothing. He didn't blame her. She was a healthy young girl. He was a middle-aged man, an unhealthy man.

Maybe she was afraid of catching the 'baker's dermatitis' that so often plagued his arms. Then there was his stomach ulcer. He'd confided in Lexy about that. Oh, how he must have bored the girl.

She had been more than patient with him.

No, he couldn't blame her. He was a fool! A bloody big fool!

Hannah was right. He was as mad as a hatter!

'You're mad!' she had bent over his chair and informed him quietly yet with dark triumph. 'I knew it. May the good Lord have mercy on your soul.'

She had been on at him for ages about his long silence, the moods of depression that alternated with wild bouts of temper. Then eventually, the day after Catriona's wedding in fact, she had, unknown to him, called in the doctor.

Lying in bed that morning, his mind roaming helplessly back over his life and all the things he regretted doing and all the things he wished he had done instead, he heard the knock on the outside door, the footsteps, and the whispering in the lobby.

Then, suddenly, into the bedroom marched Hannah followed by a young man, old Dr Grant's new assistant.

The shock, on top of the sleepless morning, after the long hard night's work, paralysed him to begin with.

He had never uttered a word while the doctor examined him, a confident young whipper-snapper with a whole lot of complicated new-fangled ideas; he had even started in a dazed faltering voice to answer some of the man's questions. It was only when Hannah began butting in and answering the questions for him that the realization of what was going on made his emotions burst alight and flame up until they almost consumed his body as well as his brain.

He'd leapt out of bed, sending the doctor sprawling and chased Hannah all through the house in his night-shirt bawling abuse at her at the pitch of his voice.

The young doctor quickly recovered and, like something out of a Charlie Chaplin film, had joined in the chase. Even when the eager beaver received a black eye for his trouble, he had, it must be admitted, taken it very well.

There had been no malice in his voice when he had recommended a psychiatrist.

Rab squirmed inside. He'd heard it said that in America nobody thought a thing about going to these headshrinkers but in his part of the world it was unheard of. A psychiatrist was the luxury of the rich hypochondriac, and the necessity of the madman.

He sighed the past away and stared bleakly ahead at the future.

First a holiday up at Montrose with Hannah's Aunty Flora and Uncle Dougal who went to bed at eight o'clock and believed that the wireless was the voice of the devil.

Then after the holiday – if Hannah had her way – the headshrinker.

Slowly he raised his face. He glowered at Hannah.

'You'll have me in the asylum yet, woman!'

'That's where you belong!'

Just in time, the doorbell saved her.

Catriona was taken aback when she looked out the window and saw the straight-backed, ruddy-cheeked, familiar figure marching across the Main Road. Yet it was reasonable enough that her mother should wish to see her before they both left for their respective holidays.

Surely Melvin could not object to that? Still, she was glad he'd gone down to the bakehouse for Fergus's present and hoped he would be delayed there for some considerable time.

Her heart pattered with excitement at the prospect of showing off her very own home, although she still hadn't had enough time to convince herself of the reality of it.

She winged her way through the hall towards the

kitchen and her soul caught its first sniff of freedom. Her mother could have no sway over her, could take nothing away from her here.

She was free, she was safe.

Round and round she danced, light-footed, long hair swirling far out then curling back close to her.

Fergus giggled when he saw her.

'Oh!' Her cheeks burned bright with embarrassment but she laughed. 'Granny's coming to visit us. You'll be a nice polite boy for Granny, sure you will?'

'Won't!'

'For goodness' sake, why not? I'll make tea and you can have some, or milk if you'd rather. And there's still some of Mrs Gordon's scones left.'

'Want to go to bed!'

'But, Fergus, I'd like you and Granny to be friends with each other.'

'Want to go to bed!' His toe poked the rug, then dug into it, then kicked it. 'Don't want a granny. Don't like a granny!'

Harassment quickened and sharpened her voice.

'Oh, all right. Go to bed, I don't care.'

Guilt flashed across her face but the problem of her mother's loud insistent ring at the doorbell was far more urgent.

Perspiring with excitement now, she flicked a glance of pride around the immaculate kitchen. The sink at the lace-curtained window was sparkling white and had a red-painted cupboard underneath it. The cooker shone, too, and the grey linoleum floor. A bright red fire burned in the hearth and its warm flickering reflected under and over the table on to the kitchen cabinet.

The hall was square, far bigger and more imposing than the narrow lobby in the house at Farmbank, and of course the bedrooms and the sitting-room were, by comparison, luxurious and beautiful.

She did another little jig of joy.

Freedom! Freedom!

As soon as the front door opened, the air became charged with anxiety.

'Are you all right?' Her mother came in, gripped her by the arm and, peering closely and worriedly at her, hustled her into the sitting-room. 'You don't look all right. What has that man been doing to you?'

In the front room she put her arm round her daughter's shoulders. 'What has he been doing to you, child?'

No one was more surprised than Catriona herself at the sudden waterfall of tears that came gushing up to overflow and spurt down her cheeks. Trembling violently, she hugged close to her mother.

'The wicked villain!' Hannah was trembling too. 'Men are all the same. All they ever want is to degrade a woman. They can do anything they like – if you don't fight to protect yourself – and a woman is at a terrible disadvantage, especially if a man gets her tied down with children. A woman has only one weapon to defend herself, and that weapon, Catriona, is her tongue. Oh, it's a man's world! You're beginning to find out what that means, no doubt. May the good Lord help and protect you!'

Hannah firmly disentangled herself, led the shivering girl over to the settee and pushed her down among the cushions.

'You wait there. I'll go through to the kitchen and make you a nice hot cup of tea.'

Visions of Melvin returning to find Hannah making herself at home in his kitchen came to sweat fear through every pore.

'No . . . I'm . . . I'm . . . I'm . . . all . . . right . . . m . . . m . . . Mummy!'

'Put your feet up!' Hannah grabbed Catriona's feet and heaved them up on to the settee for her.

'But . . . m . . . m . . . Mummy!'

'Just you relax and don't worry. I hope you're remembering to say your prayers. All this is a punishment for something you know. God has strange ways of working. Lie back. Don't move! I'll be back with a hot drink to revive you in a minute.'

The tears opened the flood-gate of emotion that had been held back by the shock of recent happenings.

She felt ill. She was glad to be lying down on the settee. She didn't think she could conjure up enough strength to stand up.

The horror of it all! She was actually, legally married, tied, in the power of a mustachioed monster of a man – for the rest of her life!

Her mother came striding back with the tea as confidently as if she owned the place.

Catriona envied her courage; especially when a few minutes later she heard the sound of Melvin's key turning and the front door opening.

'Oh . . . m . . . mu . . . mu . . . Mummy!'

'Just you keep lying there! Just you finish drinking your tea! That man won't dare say one word to you while I'm here!'

A nerve-stretching pause ensued. At long last the room door swung open, and Melvin came bumping in on his knees holding hands with a life-size monkey.

'Here we are!' he bawled. 'Ready for the Glesga Fair – wee Mickey and me!'

A stunned silence smacked over his face when his bulging eyes alighted on his horrified mother-in-law.

'Well!' Hannah was first to gather her wits together. She held her handsome head high and stared witheringly down at Melvin. 'There's more than one man in Glasgow needs to see a psychiatrist!'

Sarah just kept pushing herself on as if nothing had

happened, as if she still had her holiday money and the noise from Lender Lil was not filling the house.

She fixed up the ironing board and stood, with what looked to Mrs Fowler like impertinent nonchalance, with her back to the sink, a cigarette dangling from her lips, smoke drifting up and making her eyes wrinkle as she ironed her husband's clean shirts.

Mrs Fowler howled and mopped at waterfalls of tears with a big white handkerchief.

'All that money! All that money! . . . But, of course, you'd drive anybody to drink. It's all your fault. My Baldy never did anything like this when he lived with me. Look at you – you're a disgrace. It's time somebody forced you to be decent. You're coming with me and you're going to stay at my place in Rothesay. You're going to do as you're told for a change and no more of your snash, Sarah Sweeney!'

'Sarah Fowler. Fowler! Ah'm sorry, hen, but if ah gave you an inch you'd take a mile. And if you think ah'm goin' to crush in with you you've another think comin'.'

'Fancy! Talking to me like that. You!'

Sarah removed her cigarette so that she could bend her mouth into a smile.

'Aye, just fancy the three of us in a wee single-end in Rothesay!'

'You and me in the double bed and Baldy on the couch, what's wrong with that?'

'You'll not separate me and my man, hen.' Sarah replaced the cigarette and continued slowly and heavily with the ironing.

'I'm going through to the bathroom to wash my face.' Mrs Fowler turned to an unusually silent Baldy who was hovering huge and awkward in the middle of the floor. 'And you'd better put her in her place before I come back, do you hear? Stupid big idiot!' Her fist shot out and punched him in the ear as she passed.

Baldy's ear turned scarlet but otherwise he didn't pay the slightest attention to the assault. He made straight for Sarah as soon as his mother swept away.

'Och, come on, hen, be a sport. We might as well do as she says. Why shouldn't she spend some of her money on us for a change? The old bag's loaded.'

Sarah sucked at her cigarette and said nothing.

Baldy put a muscle-hand arm round her shoulder and gave her a squeeze.

'Will I have a word with her, then? Butter up the old cow and see if I can't get her to loaned us the money for our own wee single-end?'

'Our own wee single-end.' For a terrible moment Sarah thought she was going to disgrace herself and embarrass Baldy by bursting into tears.

Instead she puffed violently at her cigarette then managed to choke and cough out, 'You haven't a chance in bloody hell!'

'Here. She's coming. I'll catch her before she starts on you again.'

In two or three big strides Baldy covered the kitchen, bashing into and crashing over a chair in the process.

Sarah shook her head, her mouth doing its best to contort into a smile.

Out in the hall, out of Sarah's hearing, and with the thunder of the lavatory cistern in the background, Baldy met his mother.

'Bc a sport, Ma. Loaned us some money. I've enough to contend with with that dirty slut I married. Don't you let me down.'

Mrs Fowler punched him good and hard in the stomach.

'What are you blethering about? I'm offering to *give* you a holiday – pocket money and all. Don't you dare talk to me about letting folks down. What do you think you did to me when you got yourself mixed up with a useless article like that through there? You didn't need to marry her, you big fat fool! Our family's always been respectable. We've never had anything to do with the likes of Sarah Sweeney.'

She pushed past him into the kitchen, but the sudden jangle of the doorbell stopped her.

'Ah'll go,' said Sarah with a hard-core of warning behind the weakness of voice. Nobody opened the door in *her* house but her.

Tam McGuffie and Sandy MacNulty were standing there like Mutt and Jeff. Tam was only about half Sandy's size but twice as lively. His checked 'bunnet' was pulled well down on his head but he was grinning from ear to ear underneath it, and smacking and rubbing his big hands and bouncing with gleeful impatience from one foot to the other.

Sandy was grinning too and showing as much teeth and gums as Billy the horse. He was holding out his cap and shaking it, making a chinkly noise.

Tam swaggered forward.

'There you are, hen. It's from the men and the neighbours. Take it, lassie. We know you'd do the very same for any of us. Take it. Sanny'll get his cap back after.'

The cap was pushed into her hands. She clutched it to herself, lips struggling, eyes squeezing.

Tam shoved her back so that he could jerk the door shut between them.

'See you tomorrow!' he flung at her in an unnecessarily loud voice.

Sandy leaned over Tam and cried a quick word of comfort.

'You're all right now, hen!'

Then the door banged shut.

Chapter 17

The paddle steamer *Caledonia* bulged fat and weighed low down with people. Yet more and more Glaswegians were queuing up at Bridge Wharf across from the Broomilaw and crushing merrily on to swell its sides fatter and fatter.

The hot sun sparkled the vivid kaleidoscope of coloured clothes and polished brass and dazzling paint.

Already the singing had started and men were chugging bottles of whisky from jacket pockets and women were chattering and laughing and children were dashing about getting lost.

A couple of middle-aged women, their fat bouncing and wobbly before them, were facing each other up for a dance, whacking their hands, galloping towards each other, pouncing on each other's arms and uttering hair-raising 'heughs' as they birled each other round, spinning faster and faster, with everybody watching, singing and shouting, clapping hands and stamping feet.

At last the gang-planks were lifted, ropes flung aboard. The steamer gave a warning hoot and with much creaking, groaning and splashing, the *Caledonia*'s paddles were set in motion, slowly at first, the water foaming and frothing; then gradually as it rocked away from Bridge Wharf, just by the George V Bridge, the paddles quickened and found their joyous rhythm and water-churning strength.

A band began to play in the centre of the middle deck. It consisted of four men in navy-blue suits and caps. One man strummed the banjo, another had a white hanky spread over his shoulder on which rested his fiddle and his head. Another energetically squeezed and pulled at a concertina and the fourth thumped with great concentration on an ancient piano.

Melvin, Catriona and Fergus sat for'ard on the top deck because they could get all the sunshine and fresh air that was going. They also got quite a breeze and Catriona's long hair swirled and twirled and flowed out behind her.

'Make sure you enjoy every minute of this,' Melvin warned. 'It's costing me a pretty penny!'

He had not yet recovered his good humour from the previous night's débâcle with her mother.

Hannah had been either the stronger of the two personalities or the more practised in verbal warfare. Anyway, she snatched the last word before slamming away in triumph.

Long after she had gone Melvin had nagged his anger and bruised pride out on Catriona. In fact she had fallen into an exhausted sleep with his enraged voice pounding in her ears and awakened next morning to hear it, as if he had never left off, never paused for either breath or sleep.

'It's lovely.' She smiled round at him, flicking back glistening strands of hair that kept whipping across her face. 'And everybody sounds so happy. Listen to the singing!'

'Drunk, probably!' The corners of Melvin's mouth twisted, making his moustache droop low. 'They don't know how to enjoy themselves without a glass of whisky in their hands.'

The tubby *Caledonia*, brought specially up from its home-base in Gourock to help cope with the holiday crowds, waddled its cheery way past the docks, the ferries, the giant cranes jagging the sky, the ships all in different stages of growth balanced on stocks.

The yards were quiet because everything closed for the Fair. At other times when the steamers passed, the shipbuilders, swarms of men high up like ants on the sides of hulls, noisily banging and clanging, or leaning over, or up in the clouds working cranes, stopped and waved hands or caps and bawled friendly greetings.

'Haw, Bella! Why don't you buy a ship of your own?'

Today there was nothing to compete with the noisy paddle steamer except the hooting of other ships and the raucous screeching of gulls. The white-breasted birds swooped and dived alongside and followed the holiday cruises from Glasgow, knowing they were certain of generous and eagerly proffered handfuls of food right down the Clyde to Rothesay.

All the old Scots songs were getting big licks – 'Roamin' in the Gloamin', 'The Road to the Isles', 'Stop Your Ticklin' Jock', 'Ah'm The Saftest In The Family', 'I belong Tae Glasgow'. Sometimes everybody sang together, sometimes one person went solo on the verses and everyone joined with them in lusty chorus.

'Fergus!' Catriona twisted round, then stood up to squint across and round the people in an effort to see where the little boy had run off to. 'Fergus!'

'Oh, leave him alone,' Melvin growled. 'He'll be all right. Sit down!'

'He's too wee to be away on his own. He might climb up high on something and fall overboard.'

She did not wait to hear any more objections from Melvin. The child made her nervous. He behaved very strangely at times. There was no telling what he might do.

Crushing her way along the deck, she caught a glimpse of his blonde head and blue and white shirt disappearing downstairs.

'Fergus!'

No doubt the music and singing were luring him on to the other deck.

Someone was shouting.

'Come on! Come on, Jimmy lad! It's your turn. Get away from that piano, Jock. Let a Clydend man show you how it should be played. A song as well, Jimmy. Come on now! Don't be shy. We're no going to take no for an answer!'

Suddenly a cheer went up then gradually tailed away as the piano rippled into tune.

Catriona stopped half-way down the stairs, arrested by the change in the music. The piano keys were being caressed more than played and the young voice was rich and tender.

He was very handsome. Her head bent to one side to study him.

Then, unexpectedly, dark eyes flicked up and found hers.

> 'They'll be pipers down the isle,
> Bonny Mary of Argyll,
> When the heather gleams like stardust in the glen.'

A hundred voices swelled into the chorus but she could still hear his gentle tone.

'I'll be sailing down the Clyde, in my arm you'll soon abide . . .'

Held by his strangely perceptive stare, life inside her, and outside, too, acquired a new intensity, an extra dimension; the sturdy Clydebank ship, the sunbright sky, the sparkling water, the people so happily singing, everything concentrated in time, and she saw, and she heard, and she was perfectly tuned in.

Moving away to continue her search for Fergus she felt so acutely disturbed by this new awareness, the strange heightening of sensitivity, she was not sure whether it made her happy or sad.

She found the little boy and returned with him, hand-in-hand, to where Melvin was lounging back scanning a newspaper.

'He wanted to spend some of his money in the shop. I let him get an apple. I thought an apple would be better than chocolate.'

Melvin grunted from behind the paper.

Sitting beside her husband, hands clasped on lap, Catriona closed her eyes but she could still see Jimmy Gordon staring at her.

It was a good thing she enjoyed the sail 'doon the watter', Sarah told herself afterwards, because the rest of the holiday was a nightmare.

It could have been grand, and no one realized more than she did that she was lucky to have any holiday at all. She was, in fact, hoarse from thanking everybody for their help, although the money gathered barely gave them enough to cover their expenses and Baldy's pocket-money. Her gratitude knew no bounds and, hoarse or not, she continued to thank everybody she met.

If only Lender Lil hadn't spoiled the holiday. Every day in Clydend, every afternoon, regular as clockwork she nag, nag, nagged. But in Rothesay her wail never stopped from early morning until late every night. Over and over again she assured Sarah that as long as she lived she would never forgive her for accepting the 'collection' money. Water had flooded down her coarse-skinned face.

'If everybody got up collections when somebody needed money I'd be out of business. Money's my business, Miss Sweeney, in case you've forgotten! I'm a respectable business woman. I'm not in the habit of accepting charity and neither is any of my family. The Fowlers have always been respectable business folk and proud of it. You don't know the meaning of the word respectable – or pride – if you ask me!'

On and on and on, non-stop, except for the time when Baldy came in from one of his boozy dos with the lads. Usually the women, in between shopping and cooking under much more difficult circumstances than they were accustomed to at home, stuck close together on seats along the front and kept an eye on the children, and gossiped and had a laugh and did a bit of knitting and 'sooked' at ice cream.

The men very quickly found their favourite pubs and billiard halls and only emerged for food, a snore in the sun and some loving.

Baldy steered well clear of her during the day and she certainly didn't blame him, with his mother sticking to her side like a weepy crocodile. No man could be expected to spend his holidays listening to a nagging wet-eyed woman, so the only place she saw anything of Baldy was in bed where he energetically made up for lost opportunities.

The worst of it was, she had never managed to recover from the state of shock she had been whirled into before she left Glasgow. The change of surroundings and routine only made matters worse. Her mind and emotions felt as confused and bruised as her body. Never before had she been more vulnerable, never before had she been at such a disadvantage, in both preventing herself from drowning in Lender Lil's tears, and coping with Baldy's needs as a husband.

Defences down, she knocked about in a maze, stumbling miraculously from one day to the other, forgetting things, unable to concentrate, unable to hold things, continuously surprised at articles falling from her fumbling fingers. Little curtains came down over time and peering desperately back she could not see through them, could not prise open her mind to find out what she had done yesterday, or what had happened only a few hours before. Sometimes, to her secret shame, she could not even recall her own name.

All she could do was to keep automatically thanking everyone, and to smile her gratitude.

Free of the all-pervading flour that powdered his black hair and brows and long lashes, whitened his already pale skin, and dusted his clothes and shoes, Jimmy looked a new man. His hair had a gloss and seemed full of vitality. The fresh air had whipped colour to his cheeks and his eyes were brighter and shinier and more eager to find life and enjoy it than ever.

He explored Dunoon on his own and he enjoyed the aloneness as intensely and with as much appreciation as he did everything else.

His mother had soon settled down to her usual routine with her two unmarried sisters in their little house not far from the pier. She was perfectly happy to blether with them over endless cups of tea or go visiting Aunty Jeannie and Aunt Maggie's friends to have more blethers and more cups of tea.

'Och, away you go, son,' she told him in reply to his first polite offer to escort them around. 'It's no good for young laddies to be hanging about old women. Thanks, all the same, but never mind us. You get away on your own and enjoy yourself.'

Gratefully, he had escaped to walk for miles, shoulders back and – once he was away in lonely deserted places – breathing deeply in through his nose and out through his mouth in accordance with instructions in a book he had picked up at one of the book barrows in Renfield Street.

It had made fascinating study into the wonders that could be accomplished by proper breathing, exercises and self-discipline.

The self-discipline was the bit that worried him . . . the self-discipline. All his life there seemed to have been a tussle going on inside him for one reason or another. Take smoking. He reminded himself of the old joke, 'Of course I can stop smoking, I've done it hundreds of times!' The torments he put himself through trying to do without a cigarette – the torments, the depths he sunk to in defeat were just as bad, every bit as bad. After three or four days of wild pacing about and even wilder piano playing, he reduced himself to searching every pocket and ashtray in the house for dog-ends. It was always Sunday. The shops were always shut.

His mother would reprimand him. 'Saints preserve us, son, go and borrow some cigarettes from Sarah and don't stop smoking again. I can't relax when you're prowling about the place: you're like a caged tiger, laddie. You'll do more harm to yourself like this than by smoking, I'm thinking.'

Every time he persuaded himself that she was right; emotional strain was very bad for his heart. Gratefully, he rushed to have a glorious puff at one of Sarah's cigarettes. Immediately he took it he despised himself for his lack of will-power. Despised himself. He determined, if it was the last thing he ever did, the last thing, he'd master this smoking business. He just would not be beaten.

After the holidays, he would definitely give it up.

Scrambling up the Castle Hill after one of his walks he flung himself down for a rest and, propping himself up on his elbows, chewed a blade of grass as he gazed down at the pier and listened to the kilted piper playing one of the steamers away.

'Will ye no come back again?' the pipers lamented.

'Oh, we're no awa' tae bide awa',' the crowd on the ship lusitily sang, 'we're no awa' tae leave ye. We're no awa' tae bid awa' – we'll aye come back and see ye!'

Jimmy's gaze roamed across the shimmering water, back to the hills, then round to the rock on which stood the statue of Highland Mary, looking towards the coast of Ayrshire, where she met Robert Burns.

Highland Mary – Mary Campbell of Dunoon who went to work as a dairymaid or a nursemaid in Ayrshire, fell in love with the poet and, according to some people, married him 'Scotch style' by exchanging Bibles over running water.

He wondered if there were any connections between

Highland Mary and the 'Bonny Mary of Argyll' of the song.

As he stared at the state of the woman so beloved by Burns, a sadness seemed to reach out to him.

He took a deep breath to chase the sadness away. Then he felt in his pocket for a cigarette.

As soon as he returned to Clydend, he automatically reminded himself, he was going to give up smoking.

Chapter 18

All the talk after the holidays was centred round Sadie Dawson's wedding. Slasher had long ago become sick to his back teeth of hearing about it but the women customers crowding into MacNair's for their daily supply of bread and groceries could not hear enough.

They knew, of course, that it was to be in the house, although how the house was supposed to hold the huge mob that was going was anybody's guess. MacNair's were supplying the food: steak pie, potatoes and peas, Scotch trifle, assorted cakes and biscuits and – the *pièce de résistance* – the three-tiered wedding cake with a tiny bride and a little model to represent Sadie's 'intended' perched on top under an intricate arch of icing-sugar. The cake was so big, old MacNair couldn't find a box to fit it.

The street outside the shop was deserted except for Billy the horse, Sandy McNulty's van, and a mucky-faced boy of about seven called Erchie who was always hopefully hanging about with the – to old MacNair – infuriatingly persistent cry of, 'Mister, mister, any broken biscuits, mister? Hey, mister, any broken biscuits? Any stale cookies, eh?'

The only other apparent life in Dessie Street was approaching with leisurely gait from the faraway end in the form of Arthur Begg's horse-drawn coal-cart. Arthur wore a greasy cap back-to-front on his head and a leather saddle-like cape to protect his shoulder-blades, but all that could be seen of Arthur himself was the bulging whites of his eyes.

Cupping his coal-black hand round his ear when he yelled his wares, he looked as if he were trying to catch what he was saying, which was not really surprising as everyone recognized his cry but no one understood a word of it.

'Co-o-ee any o-o-o-ee f-o-o-ee Co-o-ee!'

Arthur's mare plodded slowly along, the cart rattling and groaning behind her as she stopped automatically at each close, eyeballs rolling, white-showing, the same as Arthur's.

Inside MacNair's there was first an awesome silence when the wedding cake appeared, carried with great difficulty by old Duncan and Sandy, then the silence exploded into generous and noisy praise.

Old Duncan always insisted on carrying wedding cakes out through the shop into the van so that he could bask in the reflected glory of the exquisite confections. It was, after all, his bakery and his material and his employee who had made them.

Although he'd been chiding himself all morning for having anything to do with the wedding – 'God knows when I'll get paid for all this. Everybody in Clydend lives off me after the Fair. Nobody's got a halfpenny to their name. It's just tick, tick, tick, all the time.'

None of his grumbles dampened the excitement, however.

Jimmy and Lexy came through from the bakehouse to hover proudly in the background.

'Keep back! Keep back!' MacNair sounded as if he had a peg clipped over his nose. 'Out of my road, the crowd of you.' He staggered along at an awkward angle because he was trying to prevent his whiskers from touching the cake and also because Sandy, holding the other side of the huge pillared masterpiece, was so much taller.

The customers obediently made way, still singing praises.

'Oh, isn't it lovely! Sadie's a lucky girl, so she is!'

'It's a rer cake, but! I'n't it, but?'

With much grunting and sweating and agonizing warnings to take care and not bump into anything, they managed to ease their precious burden into the van.

Dixon Street where the cake was to be delivered was only five or ten minutes away, the other side of Dessie Street from Starky Street, but MacNair had no intentions of taking any chances.

'There's tissue paper in the shop. I'll pack some round it. And where's wee Eck? Tell him to sit in the back and hold on to it in case the Benlin hooter goes and that stupid nag bolts.'

'Billy's no stupid, anything but!' Sandy puttered indignantly. 'It's very clever of him to know what that hooter means.' With long stiff legs he stalked the old man back into the shop. 'Anyway the hooter's not due for hours yet.'

Seven-year-old Erchie, his small fists pushed deep into his ragged trousers, watched them emerge from, then return to, the shop. His pace changed to a brisk skip, ever-hopeful of success in persuading the old man to give him something to eat.

Near the doorway, however, his skip slowed to a gawky stop and his mouth fell open. A fascinating horrifying scene was being enacted before his eyes.

Begg the coalman's horse was trying to take a bite out of Mister MacNair's cake.

Erchie suddenly recovered his wits and flew into the shop.

'Hey, mister, mister!'

'Get away. You wee nyaff!' the old man whined. 'Can you not see I'm busy?'

'But, mister . . .'

'I'll mister you.' He made a swipe at the child's ear but Erchie, well-practised in the art of dodging blows, proved too quick for him.

'But, mister . . .'

'I haven't got any broken biscuits, or stale cookies, you dirty-faced wee devil.'

Erchie danced up and down with exasperation. 'The coalman's horse is eating your weddin' cake.'

'What?' Knees lifting, boots clattering, old Duncan beat everybody to the door.

The coal-horse, its wide, soft mouth placidly chomping, stared round at him in innocent surprise as he burst from the shop shaking fists and screaming.

'I'll murder you. You big fat thief!'

'Who's a big fat thief?' Arthur Begg emerged from the next close, took in the scene at a glance and dived in front of his horse, arms outstretched to protect it against all comers. 'Don't you dare lay a finger on my Nellie.'

'Lay a finger on her!' Duncan howled, wildly fighting to prise Arthur out of the way. 'I'll punch the big fool until she's unconscious.'

'Over my dead body!' Arthur rolled white eyeballs in a black face held high, chin shoved aggressively forward. 'Put up your dukes!'

'Right! Right!' Old Duncan's goatee beard bristled with fury as he rapidly arranged himself into suitable fighting pose. 'I dare you, you fat mucky-faced messin'!'

He was saved from the powerful force of the coalman's fist only by the timely intervention of Jimmy who pushed his way through the magically gathered crowd – one minute the street had been empty, the next it was packed – and grabbed both Duncan and Arthur by the scruffs of their necks and jerked them away from each other.

'What are you fighting for?' Jimmy's white coat and long white apron made a startling contrast to the coalman's black clothes and the khaki-coloured shop-coat old MacNair wore. 'Look, Nellie's only taken one wee bite off the top, one wee bite, and that's only icing. Come on, help me get it back into the bakehouse. I'll soon sort it!'

* * *

Puffing at a cigarette, smoke wafting up over her blonde, bescarfed head, Sarah had gone through to stare out of the front-room window in an effort to escape Lender Lil's tongue.

It was no use.

'You've nothing better to do, I suppose, but smoke my money away and stand around poking your nose into other folks' business.'

'I don't know anything about your money,' Sarah repeated automatically, 'I don't know what you're talking about, hen.'

She leaned her brow against the window, her tired eyes resting down on the street.

The wedding cake was beautiful. It reminded her of the cake Baldy had made for their wedding. Baldy had insisted on making the cake himself. And had he been proud of it!

She tried to smile but even thinking of weddings strained her dangerously near to tears now. Emotion seemed to be building up inside her and losing its balance. Coupled with pain it was almost too much for her, nearly blotting out reason and swamping what little ability she had left to organize her resources.

More and more she longed for help and more and more she thought of the panel of doctors that sat in the converted shop they used as a surgery along the Main Road – the 'surgery yins' she called them to distinguish them from the 'hospital yins' because she already had so much to do with both. The cost of her previous visits was a shameful source of guilt that Lender Lil never allowed her to forget.

'You'll be the ruination of this family, Sarah Sweeney!' she kept saying, over and over again.

Mixed up with her need for the surgery yins was a secret sense of awe of all those in authority, people like doctors, schoolteachers, the clergy and the police.

The surgery yins and the hospital yins were important and busy men, and she shrank from bothering them and taking up any more of their valuable time in case they lost patience with her and accused her of being a nuisance.

Just as important was the fact that she had so much to do and organize before she could make a visit to the surgery.

She would have to have a bath and shampoo her hair and wash and iron all her underwear, indeed, attend to all her clothes in case she was suddenly despatched to hospital again. She'd have to go up town to buy a new nightie. She would have to see to all Baldy's clothes, too, and leave everything right for him. The house would have to be cleaned and extra shopping done; a thousand and one jobs would need to be seen to.

Even a visit to the surgery became immensely complicated, an impossible feat, once her thoughts attempted to grapple with it.

She longed to confess the terror that was emerging from the back of her mind like a monster to swim free with the upsurge of emotion.

She hardly dared turn her inward eye on the thought. Yet it was there, refusing to go away.

'Sarah, hen, you've got cancer!'

She had no clear idea of what cancer meant but it was what made Lender Lil and all the older women drop their voices to hoarse frightened whispers.

'They say it's – cancer! She's suffering agonies. She hasn't got a chance!'

The name 'cancer' was only mentioned by the more sturdy like Lender Lil. Most folk couldn't bring themselves to speak it out loud; instead it was darkly hinted at, as if they were afraid that the word itself had strange powers and was in some way infectious.

It was associated with vague but nonetheless horrible tales of women having their breasts cut off and their insides cut out so that they were left sexless, no longer real women that their men could love.

She felt ashamed; ashamed of the ever increasing untidy and dirty condition of her house and of herself, ashamed of her lack of energy, ashamed of her inability to cope. Now her shame was spreading, mingling with terror, and entering into dark unmentionable places.

Clinging tenaciously to normal comforting little routines and habit patterns she eased herself away from the window, her emaciated body like a half-shut knife, and made a slow, shuffling, agonizingly painful progress towards the other end of the house; the kitchen, the warmth of the fire, her favourite chair with the soft velvet cushion, a cup of tea in her favourite cup with the roses round it.

'The kettle's on at low.' Her voice came out little more than a whisper so she cleared her throat and tried again once she and her mother-in-law arrived through in the kitchen. 'Fancy a cup of tea, hen? I'm making one.'

'It's about all you can do, you dirty slut. The whole day long you're making yourself cups of tea. Never you mind tea just now! When I came into this house I had five pounds in my bag. Five pounds for my messages. Now it's gone and I'm not leaving here until you hand it over. You'll not do me for money, Sarah Sweeney. By God, you'll not take my money from me. That's going too far!'

Ring-a-ring-a-roses. A game she used to play as a child came unexpectedly back to her. All the wee girls joined hands together and went skipping round in a circle.

> Ring-a-ring-a-roses,
> A pocketful of posies,
> Atishoo! Atishoo!
> We all fall down!

'I don't know what you're talking about, hen.'

The cups were dirty, jammed in among a pile of pots and pans, of breakfast dishes and cutlery.

Sarah felt confused.

It wasn't nearly time for dinner yet. Lender Lil never came until dinner-time or afterwards, after she had done her shopping.

No, it wasn't nearly dinner-time yet.

They had barely finished breakfast.

She had given her man a good breakfast this morning.

There was the porridge pot, and the empty cream jug. There was the frying pan, the ham-grease hardened over crumbs of fried bread and shiny remnants of egg-whites.

'You know all right, you just haven't got the guts to look me straight in the eye and admit it.'

There was the empty marmalade jar and the small plates sticky with bread-crumbs.

The small plates had roses round them.

Ring-a-ring-a-roses,
A pocketful of posies,
Atishoo! Atishoo!
We all fall down!

Sarah smiled.

'Smirk at me, would you?' The voice suddenly gathered momentum like a train hurtling towards a tunnel. 'You impertinent article! You slut! Give me back my money or I'll strip the dirty rags off you and search them.' Her fist beat on Sarah's shoulder. 'You're a thief, Sarah Sweeney. A thief! A thief!'

Sound swelled up from inside and outside, and met, and made a mockery of the walls.

All the noise of a lifetime gathered and jabbled about.

The Benlin riveters, crowding inside high hulls, became frenzied. Trams rumbled and clanged and vied with the shipyards. Women called shrilly to each other. Men bawled and laughed and cursed and kicked balls. Children chanted. Somewhere a baby screamed. Suddenly Sarah screamed too.

Too rapid for thought, her hand darted out, grabbed a knife, whisked round and caught Mrs Fowler in the neck.

'Shut it! Shut it! Shut it!'

Mrs Fowler fell down.

Sarah stared at her.

Lender Lil was lying quietly on the floor.

Atishoo! Atishoo!
We all fall down!

An old woman lay on the floor in a heap.

'Poor soul!' Sarah murmured.

A noise at the door made her turn round. Baldy had come crashing into the kitchen in his shirt-tail.

'What the hell's going on?'

He froze at the sight of Sarah holding a blood-stained knife and his mother's body at her feet. Then he shrank, lost size as well as colour; everything about him squeezed smaller, until he was a pathetic creature trembling violently inside a too-big shirt. His legs began to buckle under him and he staggered, hands outstretched to grip the back of a chair for support.

Sarah rushed, arms ready to assist him, but like a wee boy he cried out in distress:

'Keep away from me. You've killed my mammy!'

Sarah looked down at the old woman again and in doing so noticed the knife. Opening her hands, she dropped it, waves of horror lapped away out, far out beyond her mind. She groped for something, anything she could do for Baldy before the tide came in.

'Go and get dressed, lad. Aye, that's what to do. We don't want folks seeing you like that, eh?'

'Then I'll have to go and get somebody. Oh, Jesus!' Baldy was muttering dazedly to himself. 'I'll go downstairs and tell Melvin. He'll know what to do. Oh, Jesus!'

'Go and get dressed, lad. Aye, that's what to do!'

Sarah wanted to remain where she was, thinking nothing, seeing nothing; only love of her man moved her on, and the instinctive knowledge, as yet unlinked with emotion, that maybe there wouldn't be much time left for loving him.

She followed Baldy out into the hall but when he floundered, still muttering instructions to himself, into the bedroom, she tiptoed to the front door.

She was the one who ought to tell Melvin. Baldy had done a hard night's work. He ought not to be upset. He mustn't be faced with the shameful ordeal of going downstairs to tell Melvin what she had done.

The waves were creeping closer as she clung to the iron banister, her feet hastening, stumbling down the spiral stairs. The waves rippled near, then receded with the assurance that nothing had happened. It was only a nightmare. Then they surged nearer to make her stomach heave and flutter, then disappeared again far into distance.

Melvin's wife opened the door and stared at her with huge eyes registering first a look of shy enquiry, then alarm.

'Your apron! There's blood! You've hurt yourself!'

Bewildered, Sarah stared down at herself, then up at Catriona.

'Ah've kil't Baldy's mammy!'

Different emotions scrambled over Catriona's face, changing and re-changing, jumbling senselessly together in panic. She jerked back, nursing her hands as if she'd been stung.

'Oh, no! Oh, no! Oh, what'll I do? Oh, how awful! Oh, but look at you! Oh, you poor thing. Come in just now. Come into the hall before anybody sees you.'

Sarah shuffled obediently in but her face creased and twisted.

'I'm sorry, hen,' she apologized. 'Ah didn't mean to put ye to any trouble.'

'It's all right. I mean, don't worry about me. Wait there a minute. My mother's in. We were through in the front room having tea. My mother'll help you. You'll be all right. Don't worry. Just stand there a minute.'

She pushed the front door shut, her eyes still clinging with a mixture of horror and anguished pity to Sarah's bent, old-woman figure barely discernible now in the shadow of the hall except for the grey luminous face under the woolly headscarf and the fingers poking from thick woolly mittens.

Catriona flew into the front room and babbled out a rapid stream of words to her mother.

'It's Sarah Fowler from upstairs. You remember, the poor soul that cried so much at my wedding. She's in a terrible state. She says she's killed somebody. I think she means her husband's mother. Oh, Mummy, talk to her, do something! Pour her a cup of tea while I waken Melvin. Yes, a hot sweet drink, that's good for shock. She's in a state of shock. She looks as if she doesn't know what's happened. She's waiting in the hall. I'll bring her through.'

'You'll do no such thing!' Hannah Munro managed to keep her voice down to a desperate hiss. 'Get that madwoman out of here! Get her out. Get her out before she murders the lot of us!'

For a moment Catriona's face froze in its expression of distress, then suddenly she burst into reckless speech again.

'You hypocrite! Hypocrite! Call yourself a Christian? Is this Christianity? What good's your Christianity if it's just a lot of talk?'

'Get rid of her, you fool! Get her out of the house before she murders us all.' Hannah was on her feet now, ruddy cheeks livid.

Catriona turned in a flurry of despair and darted back to the hall where Sarah was still helplessly waiting.

'I'll waken Melvin. No, my mother can tell Melvin. I'll help you upstairs. I'll make you a cup of tea.' She raised her voice. 'Mummy, tell Melvin! Tell him at once!'

She put an arm around Sarah, helped her out of the house and half-carried her back upstairs.

Sarah twisted round towards her, a pulse in her face pulling, throbbing, twitching, fluttering uncontrolled and uncontrollable.

'Ah'm terrible sorry, hen. Honest ah am. Ah'm that sorry for putting everybody to all this trouble!'

Chapter 19

Catriona sat at the kitchen table, hands balled on lap, head lowered. Opposite her, Fergus was kneeling up on his chair, his elbows resting on the table, his face cupped in his hands, watching her.

Melvin and Hannah sat on opposite sides of the kitchen fire.

'I'll never get over that as long as I live,' Hannah told Catriona for the umpteenth time. 'And the way you talked to me! I thought you'd gone off your head as well.' Her eyes rolled back to Melvin. 'And when I discovered she'd gone back upstairs with the murderess – may the good Lord forgive the poor woman – I nearly died!'

Melvin glowered.

'I told her to keep herself to herself. I told her not to have anything to do with the neighbours. I warned her especially about Sarah Fowler.'

'You needn't talk. If it hadn't been for you, she would never have been here, never got mixed up in any of this and I would never have come near the place either.'

'Nobody asked you to come.' Melvin stuck his face aggressively forward. 'But you've been here every day since we got married except for the holidays, and I suppose if you could have managed it you would have been with us then, too.'

'Yes, I would, I certainly would. I said from the beginning that no good would come of that girl coming here. I've good neighbours in Farmbank, kindly decent folk, but I told Robert – Clydend's one of the toughest districts in Glasgow, I said. I wouldn't live there and neither will that girl. But would he listen to me? Would he? Oh, no, not him! And now look what's happened. She's mixed up with a murder! A *murder*!'

'Well, it's all over now so for God's sake stop going on about it.'

'All over? All over? What about the trial? And have you looked at that street down there? It's packed with sightseers.'

'It's nothing of the kind. There's a policeman moving everybody on.'

'Oh, yes, and we know where all the folk keep moving to. Into MacNair's shop, that's where they go. You're doing all right. You don't care.'

Melvin grabbed his pipe and tobacco pouch from the mantelpiece.

'You don't know what you're blethering about. I don't own the shop. I just manage the bakery for my father. I just get a wage like everybody else. Go and gripe to the old man if you've anything to say about how much money's coming in.'

'And that dreadful man – her husband – he's still there!'

'He didn't kill the old woman. Sarah did.'

'But he's insisting that it was him who took the money, borrowed it, he says, calm as you please. If I know anything about men, it's been all his fault!'

'Calm? Baldy? He's nearly demented. Do you not know anything about murders?'

'What a stupid question!' Hannah rolled her eyes. 'As if I'd want to know anything about such things.'

'Well, you ought to know that it's quite common to have people confessing to crimes when somebody's already been arrested. It happens all the time. In Baldy's case, he's obviously putting up a desperate fight to save his wife. No wonder the police won't believe him. It's pathetic.' He jerked his head towards Catriona who was still sitting in silence, eyes riveted on motionless hands, hypnotized. 'She told you what Sarah said to the police when they questioned her – "Ah stole Lil's money. Ah'm a thief." She kept repeating it over and over again so it's an open and shut case. It doesn't matter what Baldy does now. They'll hang her!'

For the first time Catriona looked up.

'Don't say that!'

'No,' Hannah agreed. 'You shouldn't talk about these things. You'll only upset her. Don't worry, child. The poor woman's mad. They'll lock her away in an asylum. Something has to be done to protect decent, law-abiding folk from people like that, but there's no need to talk about it.'

'What's the good of acting like ostriches? Murder with theft,' Melvin insisted. 'They'll hang her. And quite right too. Murderers are nothing but a menace. Whether we like it or not we've got to get rid of them. They're no use.'

'Sarah's no use?' Catriona echoed. 'Is that all there is to say about her.'

'Aw, shut up! There's been far too much emotional guff about the bloody murderer. It's always the same. What about the victim? Nobody ever bothers about the victim!'

'I saw her lying there. I'll never forget her as long as I live. But what good is killing Sarah going to do? It won't bring Lil Fowler back.'

'Well? Tell her!' Melvin cocked a head in Hannah's direction.

'Tell her what?' Hannah asked.

'An eye for an eye, and a tooth for a tooth! By rights she should get the same as she gave. Somebody should stab a knife into her throat!'

'Be quiet!' Catriona rose, shaking so much that the table rattled under her hands. 'Fergus, go through to the bedroom, please.'

'What are you picking on him for?' Melvin gaped with astonishment. 'What has he done?'

'He's a child. He shouldn't be listening to all this. He'll be having nightmares. Fergus, go through to the bedroom I said!'

'Stay where you are!' Melvin's voice coarsened. 'I give the orders in my house.'

Hannah gave a high-pitched sarcastic laugh. 'Would you listen to the conceit of the man. Well?' Her eyes prodded Catriona to speak again. 'Are you going to let him away with it, child?'

'Mummy, please!' She was sweating now, the table-cloth under her hands wet and sticky. She was shaking so much she was terrified that she was about to take a stroke. 'I don't need you to . . . to force words into my mouth, and I'm not a child.'

'You don't need me? That's what that evil man has been putting into your head, is it?'

'For God's sake,' Melvin groaned.

Hannah rose up. 'Look at him. Listen to him. If you don't realize what a coarse, selfish, vain brute he is, then you're a fool and I pity you!'

'But, Mummy!'

Melvin levelled his pipe at her. 'Will you stop that, you stupid, stuttering ninny! You're bumping my good table and making scrape marks on the linoleum.'

'Listen to him!' Hannah jerked on her gloves and snatched up her handbag in readiness to leave. 'Never in all the years we've been married has your daddy talked to me like that. I'm sorry for you, Catriona. You're not fit to cope with that man. The moment you married him you began making a stick to break your own back. He'll be the death of you yet that man. As God's my maker, I swear it. That man doesn't care about you or anybody else. All that man cares about is himself.'

Melvin aimed his pipe at Hannah. 'Get out of my house!'

'I'm going.' Hannah glanced haughtily round at him. 'But only because I'm good and ready to go.'

'And don't come back!'

'I'll come back as often as my daughter needs me. She'll need me, all right. The poor child obviously doesn't realize what she's got herself into.'

'I'll see you to the door, Mummy.'

'Stay where you are!' Melvin bellowed. 'You belong to me now, and you'll do as I tell you.'

Hannah let out another tinkle of sarcastic laughter.

'For goodness' sake! And here was me thinking your kind of Scotsman was dying out! You're needing to be taught a few lessons, my lad. You're needing to be brought up to date.'

Despite her mother's merry tone, it was obvious that underneath the haughty manner she was flustered. Her heart was visibly palpitating, and her ruddy cheeks looked hot. Catriona couldn't help admiring the older woman's courage and silently reviled herself for her own weakness, as she remained leaning on the table and allowed her to walk alone into the hall and away from the house.

She longed to run after her and beg forgiveness.

Melvin settled back to fill his pipe.

'Thank God that's got rid of her!'

Catriona's rage rushed up and out like boiling lava. 'Don't you dare speak about my mother like that. Especially in front of Fergus. And don't raise your voice to me and order me about. Don't you dare! Don't you dare!'

'You know,' calmly Melvin lit a match, held it to his pipe and puffed a few times, 'you look positively ugly.'

Her eyes immediately lowered. She sat down, her hands clasped in her lap.

'You're not much of a housewife, either, are you? My Betty used to have every floor in this house and every stick of furniture shining like a new pin. A good skin of polish protects things. Didn't you know that? Polish protects and takes care of things and makes them last. You've got to use some elbow grease, of course. You've got to put on a good skin.'

'And, Daddy!' Fergus's high-pitched childish voice interrupted. 'My porridge was cold this morning.'

Melvin jerked forward in his chair, pipe forgotten.

'Do you hear that? His porridge was cold. What do you mean by it? What excuse have you got?'

Catriona looked up.

'An old woman has been murdered. A young woman, a neighbour of ours, is in danger of being hanged. And you ask me what excuse I have for letting Fergus's porridge get cold?'

'Aw, shut up! What happens to the Fowlers is their business. Your business is to attend to this house and me and my son.'

Catriona lowered her eyes and said no more, but she had learned something important.

She now knew how Sarah Fowler must have felt and how easy it would be for anyone to feel like committing murder.

Jimmy made his way slowly up the stairs. His face showed signs of strain. Thoughts of Mrs Fowler, of Sarah and of Baldy who was now practically living night and day in the bakehouse and talking desperately and incessantly about his wife and the trial – worrying thoughts were driving him to distraction. During the day while he worked, and tossing and turning and sweating in bed during the night, vivid three-dimensional pictures in realistic colour whirred and whirled through his mind, horrifying beyond all horror.

Fear for Sarah's fate jostled with anger and the intensity of his suffering for neighbour and friend. A thousand times in his imagination he was with her in Duke Street prison, a thousand times he made the imaginary walk with her to the scaffold.

He had known Sarah, Mrs Fowler and Baldy all his life.

He had not the slightest doubt that Sarah must have been strained beyond all human endurance. He had told the police so in no uncertain terms. The most terrible thing of all was that so many people did *not* know Sarah, or Baldy, or Mrs Fowler.

To strangers this appeared only as a brutal crime motivated by greed and theft, and perpetrated on a helpless old woman. A young blonde from a tough area of Glasgow had robbed a helpless old lady and when the old lady had pleaded for the return of her money the young peroxide blonde had calmly lifted a kitchen knife and stabbed her mother-in-law to death.

Letters in the papers, signed with pseudonyms like 'Off With Their Heads' and 'Vigilante' and 'Shocked', argued back and forward about capital punishment. The hate, the lust for revenge, the violence shown in some of the letters nauseated and depressed him beyond words. They talked of hanging being a deterrent. He couldn't understand why. There never had been any evidence to show that it deterred. It certainly had not deterred Sarah.

How many other Sarahs had there been, he wondered? How many Sarahs yet to come?

He stopped on the first landing, his chest tight, his breath catching in his throat.

'Are you feeling all right?' Melvin's wife was standing in her doorway, a polishing cloth and a tin of polish in her hand. She smiled a ghost of a smile at him, her eyes avoiding his. 'I'm Catriona. You're Jimmy Gordon, aren't you?'

'Yes.' He wiped his floury hands on his apron before offering her one. 'I only wish I was meeting you in happier circumstances. It's . . . It's . . .' He shook his head, words failing him.

'I know,' Catriona agreed. 'I can't sleep at night just thinking about it. That poor old woman. And poor Sarah . . .'

He was snatched back to the immediate present by the touch of her hand. He found himself staring in silence at the gentle face, his fingers tightening round her fingers, surprised by the familiarity of the warm flesh.

'I listen to you playing the piano – ' she broke the silence with a small tremulous voice. 'It's lovely.'

Their hands slid apart and Jimmy became aware of an aloneness he had never noticed before.

'Do you mean that?'

She nodded. 'Melvin has a piano in the front room. It used to belong to Betty. Nobody plays it now, though. I think it's badly out of tune.'

'I'll come down and try it sometime, if you like. See what I can do.'

'Thank you.' She blushed. 'You'll be welcome any time.'

'I love music,' he confided. 'At one time I had very grand ideas. Oh, very grand ideas. I was going to be a concert pianist. A concert pianist, no less!'

'Why didn't you?'

He hesitated, not wanting to talk of his illness in case it would decrease his manliness in her eyes, unable to explain about keeping a roof over his mother's head in case that sounded self-pitying or conceited.

'I wasn't good enough.'

'I don't believe it . . .' Quickly she looked up, her sincerity unmistakable. 'You're wonderfully talented!' Her blush deepened and she turned her attention to polishing her front door again.

'You're very kind.' He smiled, then continued his way upstairs, more intensely disturbed that ever.

Chapter 20

Duke Street Prison, official address 71 Duke Street, was a dark, long, antediluvian building with row upon row of high-up, heavily barred slits, and was bounded by a dismal wall. The jutting front gable of the building had a clock that the tram-traveller could see over the wall. The clock had never been known to go.

The prison used to be a house of correction for women 'where they may be whipped daily'. It had also seen many children punished in the past. In one year alone, there had been imprisoned in Duke Street five children under ten years of age, fifteen between the ages of ten and eleven, seventy-six from twelve years to thirteen years, and a hundred and fifty-nine prisoners in the fourteen to fifteen years-of-age class.

This was where Oscar Slater had frantically protested his innocence.

Along the west wall were tablets that marked the graves of hanged murderers. The initials of each murderer and the year of the hanging were inscribed on the tablets.

Unlike in America, the bodies of prisoners were not handed over to relatives. The reason stated in the Royal Commission report was: 'hanging leaves the body with the neck elongated'. The Home Office had stated that 'as now carried out, execution by hanging can be regarded as speedy and certain'. The Home Office was referring to a change in technique, a drop of variable length and a sliding ring which was supposed to hold the knot of the noose under the left jaw. This, they hoped, would prevent the difficulties of the past when the agony of suffocation without loss of consciousness could last up to twenty minutes, not to mention innumerable forms of mutilation: joints torn off by hitting the edge of the trap, heads partly or entirely torn off, and people having to be hanged twice and even three times in succession.

This innovation referred only to England.

When hangman Pierrepoint was questioned about the Scottish methods of hanging, he admitted: 'It is very very old, antediluvian. It is time it was altered in Scotland.'

These facts, gleaned from innumerable books, papers and authorities on the subject, milled round in Jimmy's mind as he accompanied Baldy on one of his visits to Sarah in Duke Street prison.

All the time that Baldy was talking loudly and aggressively about how Sarah was going to be all right and how he'd batter anybody to pulp with his bare hands if they even looked at her in the wrong way, Jimmy was silent, his thoughts completely swamping him.

Only the other day when he'd gone into town for his mother's prescription – she had become so worried and upset about Sarah, she couldn't sleep without taking tablets – he had overheard a snatch of conversation in the chemist's between a very respectable-looking man and woman. They had been voicing the opinion that they hoped the Fowler woman would not be hanged, although no doubt she deserved it – but, of course, they decided eventually, 'hanging is quick and clean – they don't feel anything – they never know anything about it!'

He had turned on them, eyes blazing, heart pounding like a sledgehammer in his chest, and told them exactly what hanging meant, described it to them in accurate detail, sparing them nothing.

They had been affronted and the man snorted indignantly. 'How dare you speak like that in front of a lady, you young horror! Don't you know you shouldn't talk about these things? It's not decent!'

'You made the statement,' Jimmy protested. 'You said

that hanging was quick and clean and the prisoner doesn't feel anything or doesn't know anything about it. I've only told you the facts.'

'We don't want to stand here listening to horror stories from you,' the woman raised her voice, at the same time tugging her companion's sleeve, desperate for escape. 'I don't know what this country's coming to when respectable people can't come into a chemist's shop without being pestered.'

'I've only given you the facts,' Jimmy insisted.

But the couple had stamped away from the shop in a flurry of fury. No doubt they would soon calm down over a glass or two of brandy or a nice cup of tea.

The worst of it was that while people like that were tucked safely away in their own unthinking and unimaginative little worlds, others were being allowed to *act* and, as a result, people were suffering and had suffered and would continue to suffer in a million different ways; in poverty and in ignorance and in wars, and as a result of wars, on every side, all over the world.

As soon as they entered the prison, even Baldy fell quiet. The place was incredibly gloomy and oppressive. Inside this ancient building the Sarah they knew waited under sentence of death.

A petition for reprieve had been forwarded to the Secretary of State for Scotland. The petition asked that the death sentence be commuted to penal servitude and referred to evidence of mental aberration at the time she committed the crime. Reference was also made to the jury's unanimous recommendation to mercy.

Baldy left the silent white-faced Jimmy in the gatehouse and, barrel chest stuck out, big shoulders back, gorilla-hands clenched in pockets, he strode after the prison officer who led him across the prison yard and into the main building to where he could speak to his wife.

Sarah was looking prettier than she had done for years.

Her blonde hair was brushed back and shining and she was wearing a green dress and a pink woollen cardigan.

Baldy's muscle-hard face screwed into a wink.

'You're looking great, hen. You're going to be all right, eh?'

Her face crinkled.

'Ah'm all right as long as ah've got you, sure ah am, Baldy.'

'By God you are, hen. I won't let anybody lay a finger on you. You're my wife. Are they treatin' you all right, eh?'

'Och, aye. Everyone in here's nicer than the other. They're all that kind to me. Fancy, the polis and all the high-heed yins. They're all that kind. Ye've no idea! Even the holy yin comes to chat with me. And the food's just lovely too!'

'You're all right then, hen?'

'Och, aye, don't you be worryin' yourself so much about me. You're an awful man, so you are.'

There was a pause while she gazed at him and smiled at him.

'Know something?' He suddenly broke the silence.

'What?'

'You're just like what you were when we got married, remember?'

'Aye, fine.' Her voice saddened. 'Ah haven't been much of a wife to you, lad.'

'I told you not to talk like that so shut your mouth.'

The smile tried to flicker back but her eyes had gone wistful. She hesitated, the words on her tongue longing to come out but afraid of the embarrassment and the hurt they might cause.

'Ah've always loved you though, Baldy,' she managed at last. 'Have you been fond of me, eh? I mean before . . . Ah mean, ah don't expect . . . Ah don't deserve anything now . . . And ah'm that sorry, Baldy . . . ah'm that ashamed.'

'Don't talk like that, you dope!'

'Ah've caused you nothing but trouble, ah know.'

'You're my wife!' he insisted stubbornly as if that was enough, as if that settled everything.

Melvin had let Lizzie in and then gone down to the bakehouse to check with Jimmy about how much jam and fondant and fruit and other items needed to be ordered.

Catriona, nerves ragged with lack of sleep, was left feeling very ill-at-ease with her next-door neighbour. Already Lizzie had made several complaints and accusations against her.

Only the other day after she had put out crumbs in the back court for the birds, Lizzie had limped after her with a brush and shovel, swept up the crumbs and angrily complained to her: 'I know what you're doing, you sly little minx, but you won't get away with it.'

'I have no idea,' she protested when she recovered from her initial surprise, 'what on earth you're going on about!'

'Oh, you know, all right! Don't tell any of your lies! That baby-face of yours maybe fools the men but it doesn't fool me.'

'Know *what*, for goodness' sake?' Irritation at being bothered by trivialities at such a tragic time gave her voice unusual emphasis.

'You know that I've just hung up that washing, don't you?'

'Yes, but what's that got to do with me putting out crumbs for the birds?'

'You know those birds are going to fly over my washing to reach your crumbs. You know they're going to do their filthy business on their way over. All over my clean washing. You know, all right!'

'Oh! I've never heard anything so ridiculous!'

At any other time she might have giggled, but laughter, when Sarah was lying in the condemned cell at Duke

Street prison, was something obscene. Everyone in the narrow cobbled street was talking in low-pitched whispers of voices, gathering in serious-faced crowds at corners and at close-mouths and in each other's houses.

She pushed impatiently past Lizzie and left her without uttering another word.

Now here she was again and at Melvin's invitation, to stop her thinking about Sarah no doubt.

'You're thinking and talking far too much about Sarah Fowler,' he'd exploded. 'And what you're wasting your time and mine on her for beats me. After all, whether you like it or not, the woman's a killer and she'll have to pay the penalty. She should have thought about the consequences before she carved up Mrs Fowler. She's nobody but herself to blame.' And eventually he had crushed the words of protest that came rushing to her mouth by his 'Aw shut up! Nothing you think or say or do is going to make one bit of difference. You're not the Secretary for Scotland!'

His contempt for her added flames of anger to her distress and she had tried to relieve her feelings by throwing herself into a frenzy of housework, working so feverishly at cleaning and polishing the place with such thoroughness that she felt certain he would never again be able to find any excuse to criticize her.

Yet he had been more furious with her than ever and had glowered at her and poked and peered about until, just before stamping out of the house, he'd shoved the chip pan under her nose.

'Look at that, It's a disgrace. Do you not even know how to clean a chip pan? The outside's thick with filthy grease.'

Then she had heard him muttering to Lizzie on the landing and Lizzie had limped in with a gleam in her eyes, looking very pleased with herself.

'Hello, my precious wee son.' She leaned over Fergus

who was on his way out to play in the back green. 'Here's a sixpence to buy yourself lots and lots of sweeties.'

'Lizzie, you simply must stop doing that,' Catriona gasped with annoyance. 'It just makes him sick and spoils him from eating a proper meal.'

'Huh!' Lizzie swung round and jerked up on her painful hip. 'You'll not tell me what to do, or what not to do with my own wee baby, you impertinent upstart. What do you know about my wee Fergie?'

'I know he's *not* your wee Fergie!'

Catriona immediately regretted her hasty words because she saw the wound they made before it was covered by hatred.

'How dare you talk to me like that,' Lizzie said harshly. 'You sly, wicked . . .'

'Oh, be quiet!' Irritation overcame her again. 'I'm sick of listening to your stupid talk. I'm not sly. I'm telling you straight to your face. I don't want you to keep interfering and spoiling Fergus.'

'Wait till Melvin hears about this! "Keep an eye on her and Fergus," he says. "As soon as my back's turned she'll be wandering about there like the ghost of Lady Macbeth," he says. He'll hear about this, all right. You're not fit to look after a child. What children have you ever looked after before? What do you know about children?'

'There's the door, Lizzie!'

After it slammed shut with a violence that rocked the house, Catriona covered her face with her hands.

She waited. After the noise came the silence, and after the silence, her thoughts.

Suddenly she tore off her apron, grabbed the key from its hook, flew from the empty house and pelted upstairs.

Amy Gordon, like a woman caught unawares by old age, shuffled across the hall in answer to her knock and peeked round the door, her motherly face bewildered.

'Oh, it's you, dear.' She sighed with relief. 'Come in,

come in, I'm so pleased to see you. It's awful to be alone at a time like this, isn't it?'

She led Catriona through to her front room. 'I was just sitting here having a wee rest and looking out the window. Usually I've got Baldy in but he's next door just now with half the street in beside him and I'm glad. Poor man, he's trying so hard and with so much noise to make out he's not in the least bothered, but everybody knows he's nearly demented and he's awful hard to thole. I'm exhausted with him and glad some of the others are taking a turn. You'll drink a wee cup of tea, dear?'

'No, thank you.'

'Och, just a wee cup. It'll be no bother to make and you're welcome.'

'I couldn't drink it, honestly. I just wanted the company. I knew you'd understand.'

'Yes, of course, dear. Sit down and make yourself comfy.' Mrs Gordon sighed and shook her head. 'I'm worried about Jimmy, too. He gets so worked up about everything. He gets all excited about far less important things than this, so you can imagine what he's like just now.'

'I've been speaking to him. He looks awfully pale and dark under the eyes. Has he been keeping all right? He says it's lack of sleep but nobody's getting much sleep and I suppose we all appear a bit wan. It looks more than that with him somehow . . . he seems . . . I don't know . . .' Suddenly hot-cheeked she floundered in embarrassment but words – 'His face haunts me!' – escaped before she could stop them.

Jimmy's mother was too preoccupied with her own worries, however, to notice anything out of the ordinary about her guest's tone of voice.

'The lad was so ill.' Plump hands clasped and unclasped on aproned lap. 'Before your time, dear. A few years back. Rheumatic fever it was and it left its mark on his heart. The doctor said he'd be all right as long as he took good care of himself and kept himself calm, as if my Jimmy could ever do any such thing.'

'Oh, dear!' Catriona's heart pounded louder and louder, stronger and stronger, like the beat of some fearful tribal drum, until it was shaking the very roots of her existence.

'He's got plenty of spirit,' Mrs Gordon went on. 'I agreed with the doctor about that. He said Jimmy had youth on his side too and he'd be all right but, oh, lassie, lassie, I'm awful worried about my boy. He's that fond of Sarah Fowler. She used to come in here every day and take a turn looking after him when he was ill and let me lie down for a wee sleep.

'She was that gentle with him, too, the way she used to sponge his hands and face, and he remembers, you see. She's always been such a kindly wee soul, Sarah, and aye ready with a smile or a joke. She used to have Jimmy grinning from ear to ear even while he was not able to move a muscle for the rheumatic pains.' Suddenly she stopped, her expression anxiously alerting. 'I think that's him now. Aye, he's coming through. He always makes straight for the piano every time he comes in.'

Her face acquired a forced brightness as soon as her son appeared in the room. 'Hello, son. This wee lassie's come upstairs to keep me company. Wasn't that kind? I'll go and make a cup of tea now.'

Rising she turned to smile at Catriona. 'He loves his cup of tea when he comes in.' Her smile returned to Jimmy who was standing very still, gazing across the room at Catriona. 'Don't you, son?'

He winked round at her.

'You're the best old tea-maker in Glasgow!'

'Less of the "old" I keep telling you, you rascal,' she scolded as she passed. 'Sit down at that piano and give the wee lassie a song and a tune. I won't be a minute and we'll all have a cup. It'll put some pith into us and make us feel better. There's nothing like a good strong cup of tea.'

The room was silent after she went out. Jimmy kept standing near the piano, massaging his fingers, his eyes never leaving Catriona until her cheeks flushed rose-pink.

'Please play something,' she said at last, wanting to keep the dark eyes holding hers, but terrified of the welter of emotion his penetrating stare was firing into life.

He sat down at the piano and allowed his fingers to flow over the keys before he began to speak to the music.

'I have heard the mavis singing
His love song to the morn;
I have seen the dew-drop clinging
To the rose just newly born;
But a sweeter song has cheered me
At the evening's gentle close;
And I've seen an eye still brighter
Than the dew drop on the rose.
'Twas thy voice, my gentle Mary,
And thine artless winning smile,
That made this world an Eden,
Bonnie Mary of Argyll . . .'

Chapter 21

'Sex and aggression,' Jimmy expostulated in between gulps of tea. 'Sex and aggression, beside tribal loyalty, are the most powerful biological drives.'

Hannah Munro tried not to look shocked. She had come upstairs in search of her daughter and also to wait while Rab next door took his daily (as well as nightly) turn with the rest at listening to Baldy and struggling to calm him down.

Hannah had never uttered the word 'sex' herself nor ever heard it spoken out loud – let alone in mixed company; and if Jimmy had not been such an obviously well-meaning young man she would have gathered all the dignity at her disposal and swept from the house. As it was, she remained straight-backed on the edge of her seat, sipping tea and bracing herself because she sensed, and rightly, that worse was still to come.

'And you see,' Jimmy's eyes flashed around, 'it's a question of keeping the savage inside all of us under control. Strictly controlled, you see. The sexual appetites usually find a reasonable amount of acceptable outlets but aggression has almost none. Here's where our danger lies. Lies waiting to rear up and destroy the civilized part of us. The murder trial appeals to the cruel savage hiding inside us; like a gladiator in an arena, a human being is fighting for his life and the thrill is the same as in the arena – will the thumbs go up, or down!'

'How true!' Hannah murmured, impressed despite herself. 'There's a beast in every man, right enough.'

'Now, now, son,' his mother pleaded. 'I wish you wouldn't get all worked up like that.'

'Oh, Mother, I wish everybody would get worked up.'

'Perhaps people are losing sight of the real meaning of charity.' Catriona gazed tentatively across at Jimmy, hoping she had said something that would please him, and seeing his nod of agreement, was encouraged to go on. 'Charity has come to mean just putting a few pennies in a collection box, hasn't it? But the Bible says it's much, much more than that. It says . . .'

'Yes, indeed, child,' Hannah's strong voice interrupted. 'The Good Book says: "Though I have all faith so I could remove mountains, and have not charity, I am nothing. And though I speak with the tongues of men and of angels, and have not charity, I am become as sounding brass or a tinkling cymbal."'

'Yes,' Catriona whispered and lowered her eyes. But she could still feel Jimmy's gaze on her face, warm with understanding.

Her mother and Mrs Gordon continued the conversation but their voices were like meaningless droning faraway in the background.

There was something far more powerful in the room, something silent, invisible, yet reaching out, touching, caressing the sensitive nerve ends of every secret corner of her soul.

'Bonnie wee thing,' Jimmy said very quietly. 'Cannie wee thing.'

His words, though almost a whisper, affected her like delicious electric shocks.

'Did you say something, son?' Mrs Gordon turned to him.

He smiled.

'I was asking Catriona if she knew any of the poems or songs of Robert Burns.'

'Oh, yes.' Catriona looked up, wide-eyed now, and breathless. 'I think he's wonderful.'

'Well, by jovie,' Mrs Gordon laughed. 'You and Jimmy

should get on fine. He knows his Burns off by heart.' Then, as if suddenly remembering Sarah, and feeling ashamed at having laughed, she gave a big sigh. 'Aye, he was a great man. My husband was fond of him, too. Many a Burns supper he attended. Was that the door, Jimmy? Yes, go and open it, son.'

'It'll be my husband,' Hannah said, rising. 'It's time we were away, Mrs Gordon. We'll be over again, though. It's an awful business, isn't it?'

'You'll remember poor Sarah in your prayers, Mrs Munro?'

'Yes, I will indeed. May the good Lord help and protect her. Come on, Catriona. It's time you were going too, child.'

Jimmy was talking to Rab when they reached the hall.

'Is there still somebody with him?'

Rab nodded. 'Tam and Sandy are still there and two or three from down the street. They'll stay with him until it's time for work again.'

'You're dead beat,' Hannah accused him in a comparatively friendly, almost proud tone. 'Look at the colour of your face!'

Rab's shaggy brows pushed down. The matter of the headshrinker had been relegated, swamped by the more urgent and tragic turn of events, but he had not forgotten or forgiven Hannah. 'How can I look at the colour of my face, woman? I don't go around with a mirror hanging on the end of my nose!'

Hannah rolled her eyes towards Mrs Gordon.

'Men!'

Jimmy smiled down at Catriona when the others were making their goodbyes.

'I'll play for you,' he said. 'Will you listen?'

She smiled up at him, her glowering eyes giving him his answer.

Later, not long after she returned downstairs, the house

began to echo, vibrate, fill gloriously to the rafters with Beethoven, Tchaikovsky and Rachmaninov until Melvin flung down his newspaper and bawled through his moustache at the pitch of his voice, 'Jumpin' Jesus! If it's not one damned thing it's another! Has Jimmy Gordon gone berserk now? I can't hear myself think for that bloody racket!'

'Be quiet!' Catriona burst out before she realized what she was saying. 'How can you talk like that about such wonderful music, such perfect artistry?'

'I'll talk any way I like in my own house – and since when have you been a music-lover?'

Suddenly she felt frightened, not only for herself, but for Jimmy. Her eyes avoided the angry stare now bulging with suspicion. She shrugged.

'Anything to keep my mind off the murder and that poor woman lying in Duke Street prison.'

She said the words to protect Jimmy, yet she could not bear how disloyal to his talent they sounded. She sought and found for his sake a new well of courage.

'But why shouldn't I enjoy good music if I want to? That is good music, you know, and Jimmy Gordon is an unusually talented pianist.'

'What's going on here?' Melvin got up, his voice incredulous. 'Is there something between you two?'

'Don't be ridiculous!' Catriona stood her ground, her eyes refusing to be beaten down. 'Am I not even to be allowed to listen to music?'

'You're not going to be allowed to speak to me like that!' Suddenly he flung back his head and gave an ear-splitting roar that reverberated painfully through her head.

'Jimmy, you bastard! If you don't give that bloody piano a rest, I'll come up there and kick it from here to Kingdom Come!'

The piano did not stop. It finished the piece it had been

playing. Then it began another – the different, brighter, cockier rhythm of 'Gin a body meet a body coming through the rye'.

Melvin gritted his teeth.

'Hear that! He's a determined, impertinent young bastard! I don't know why my father puts up with him. If it was left to me he would have had his cards long ago!'

Catriona kept silent though she longed to flay him with bitterness.

What a fool she had been to marry him. She realized that now. She had been far too young and her world had been smaller, more confined, more naïve than any nunnery. He had taken unfair advantage.

There were times when she tried not to blame him, when she fully accepted the responsibility herself, but this was not one of those occasions.

He had been older and far more experienced than she. He had rushed her into a loveless marriage of convenience. All he wanted was a housekeeper and someone to look after his son. He wanted sex too, of course – oh, plenty of sex and at the oddest, most inconvenient and nerve-racking times, as if he did it purposely to degrade and torment her.

There never had been any mention of love. They seldom kissed and when they did he had the peculiarly insulting habit of wiping his mouth and his moustache with the back of his hand immediately afterwards as if to remove the slightest taste of her.

'Now he's got Lexy mooning after him, the old man tells me.' Melvin relaxed back in his chair again, forgetting his suspicions. 'Nuts about him she is, and making no secret of it. What's got into her all of a sudden I haven't a clue. She's been working down there since not long after she left school and never a bit of bother and now all of a sudden she goes all cow's eyes and weak-kneed over him. It's bound to affect her work. I told the old man

– something'll have to be done about that guy. But all I get for my troubles is told to shut up. "I can manage Jimmy. You shut up and mind your own business," he squeaks at me. At *me*! The old sod's soft in the head. It's time he retired altogether.'

'Is that the girl that lives up in one of the attic flats?'

'That's her. Sexy Lexy they call her. She's a buxom piece.'

'She's pretty, isn't she?' Her voice struggled to sound casual and smother the misery underneath it. 'Is Jimmy in love with her?'

'Don't be a fool! She's as common as dirt. He's had her out, though. I'll give you three guesses what for!'

She felt sick.

'Jimmy Gordon's not like you.'

'What?' Melvin suddenly guffawed with laughter. 'I wouldn't be too sure. He's only a boy compared with me, of course. I know what women like, eh?'

She froze, terrified to move or say anything that might incite him to demonstrate his sexual prowess right there and then.

'Well?' His voice loudened. 'Don't I?'

She managed to smile.

'Betty wrote some lovely letters, I remember. She must have been very fond of you. What age was Fergus when she died?'

Hearing herself, she felt amazed. It was like someone making polite conversation with a stranger. Then suddenly she realized he *was* a stranger and, to her, he would never be anything else.

Bitterness drowned in sadness. She didn't hate him. He didn't mean any harm. There wasn't necessarily a thing wrong with him as a husband – if he had the right wife, a wife like Betty for instance. On one point she was quite certain. She was not the right wife for him. Yet she had agreed to his proposal of marriage of her own free will and had stood up in the Hall and agreed to love, honour and obey him until 'death us do part'.

Even now, she could hardly credit it.

I must have been mad, she thought.

'Oh, he was only a baby.'

'What?' Legs shaking, she groped for a chair.

'Fergus. He was only a baby when Betty died. I told you before.'

'Did you?'

'I don't think I told you about the christening, though.' He lounged back, a glaze of pride lifting his face. 'It was the best do folks round about here had been to in years. There wasn't a dry eye in this house.'

'What do you mean?'

'It was just the day before Betty died. I knew she couldn't last much longer and I wanted to do everything I could for her before the end. That was the day I sent for her girlfriend – Jenny something-or-other. I never could remember that girl's name. And I got a preacher to come and baptize Fergus and I propped Betty up on the settee in the front room and put Fergus in her arms. I invited all the neighbours to the christening. That room was packed and of course I had it looking lovely, all polished to perfection and clean curtains up and the carpet shampooed. I had given Betty a bath and bought her a new nightie and a bedjacket and brushed her hair – she had long hair the very same as you – but she was just skin and bone and she looked so pathetic and obviously not strong enough to hold the baby, so I knelt beside the settee and supported him for her while the minister conducted the service. I'm telling you there wasn't a dry eye in this house.'

Catriona sat transfixed on the chair opposite from him.

Eventually becoming aware of her silence, he eyed her curiously.

'What's wrong with you? You look as if you've seen a ghost!'

Her face crumpled.

'Come here, stupid!' He leaned forward, caught hold of her arm and dragged her across to him until she was sitting on his knee. 'There's no use crying for Betty now. I cried right enough and I'm not ashamed to admit it. I cried like a baby in front of everyone at her funeral and I've cried to myself many a time since. But crying doesn't bring anyone back. I had to face facts eventually.' He held her head down on his shoulder and stroked her hair. 'So don't cry, darlin',' he told her in the gentlest tone he'd ever used to her. 'You're my wife now. I've got you to look after now, eh?'

'Oh, Melvin!' She squeezed her fists against her mouth in an unsuccessful attempt to contain her sobbing. 'I'm frightened!'

Chapter 22

Early in the afternoon, telegrams from the Home Secretary, intimating that no reprieve had been granted, were received by the Lord Provost of Glasgow, Sir Andrew Finlay, and the town clerk, Sir Meikle Tate.

The telegram to the Lord Provost said: 'The Secretary for Scotland is unable to discover sufficient grounds to justify him in advising interference with the due course of law in the case of Sarah Fowler, now lying under sentence of death.'

No doubt Sarah's pleasant, well-balanced and co-operative behaviour before, during and after the trial had weighed heavily against her agent's plea of insanity.

Shortly after receiving the telegram, as was the custom, the Lord Provost and the town clerk proceeded to Duke Street Prison to inform the prisoner of her fate.

They were received by the governor, and Dr Stewart, and the Reverend McNeill who accompanied them in solemn, dignified procession to a room in the section reserved for women.

A female warder went to the condemned cell to fetch the prisoner.

Sarah welcomed her with a smile.

'Hallo, hen. Is it ma man come tae see me?'

'No, Mrs Fowler,' the woman said. 'It's the Lord Provost and the town clerk. Come on, I'll take you to them.'

'The Lord Provost and the town clerk?' Sarah was deeply impressed, deeply grateful. 'Would you believe it. Ah told ma man that all the high-heed yins were bein' that kind to me but ah never dreamt that anybody as high-up as the Lord Provost would come tae pay me a visit. And the town clerk, too!'

She tidied back her hair and tugged down her green prison dress and fumbled with the buttons of the pink cardigan as she accompanied the wardress along the corridor.

Entering the room she was more impressed and awe-struck than ever when she discovered not only the imposing figures of Sir Andrew Finlay and Sir Meikle Tate, but the governor, the doctor and the holy yin as well.

She cleared her throat.

'It's awfi kind o' ye all . . .'

'Sh . . . sh . . .!' the wardress reprimanded.

Sarah sucked in her lips in a gesture of embarrassed apology. Then, as if to make up for her lapse, she crinkled her face into an expression of rapt concentration on what the Lord Provost was obviously preparing to say.

'Mrs Fowler,' he began at last. 'It is with profound regret that I am obliged to be the bearer of a sad message. I am deeply sorry to inform you that the Secretary for Scotland has not seen his way to grant you a reprieve.'

Sarah's features relaxed. She looked bewildered.

She allowed the wardress to take her arm and lead her towards the door.

Then her legs buckled under her. The prison doctor rushed to the wardress's assistance and between them they supported and half-carried her from the room.

'Baldy!' The corridors began to echo with whimpers. 'Baldy!' The whimpers quavered louder. 'Baldy!'

And louder.

Until the pitiful cries for her husband were muffled by the clang of the cell door.

Jimmy paced back and forward.

'It's barbaric!' He stopped to twist out his cigarette in an ashtray. 'Barbaric!'

'Jimmy, son, please! Try to keep calm!' His mother pleated and unpleated her apron between her fingers, her anxious eyes never leaving his face.

Catriona was hovering near. Lexy was there, too.

'Calm? Calm?' He gesticulated wildly. 'How can I keep calm? They're going to strangle Sarah Fowler in the morning!'

'Ohi! Ohi! Jimmy!' Lexy's face twisted grotesquely as she burst into tears. 'Don't say that. She was always so nice to me!'

'But it's true, Lexy,' he said brokenly, and lit another cigarette.

Lexy began to wail and Mrs Gordon put an arm round her and persuaded her from the room.

'Jimmy, stop it!' Catriona blocked his way as he made to start pacing again. 'Nothing can be done now. You'll only make yourself ill.' She put a restraining hand on his arm. 'You've tried your best. You've written to the press. You've gathered petitions. You've organized pickets outside the prison. No human being could possibly have done more than you and Baldy and all Sarah's neighbours and friends.'

'Oh, Catriona! Catriona!'

'Sh . . . sh!'

Her hand tightened on him. She felt the warmth of his body and gazing up she longed to touch the thick unruly hair, the dear emotional face; to hold him close to her, caress him, soothe him with soft secret whispers, move closer and closer, melt into him, to be one with him, never to break apart.

'Catriona!'

'Sh . . . sh . . . Jimmy, love, please.'

She turned away as Mrs Gordon, accompanied this time by a red-nosed, red-eyed Sandy, came back into the room.

'Is Melvin still there?' she asked Sandy.

He nodded and his lips puttered in and out but he was, for a moment, incapable of speech.

'Sit down, Sandy.' Mrs Gordon took his arm and led him like a stiff-legged child over to a seat. 'There's tea in the pot. The wee lassie'll pour you a cup.'

'My father-in-law locked the bakery. The shop will be shut tomorrow, too.' Sandy nodded again and accepted the cup Catriona offered.

'He's still the same, is he?' Jimmy asked. 'Still the same?'

Sandy cleared his throat.

'Aye. Rab and the rest have been pumping whisky down his throat for hours and he's still stone-cold sober. Talk-talk-talking, though, as if he still doesn't believe what's going to happen. How he can keep talking at all, just keep on like that, has us all baffled. He's got us fair exhausted, that fella, and he's still going strong. He's never shut an eye once. I'm dreading the morning for more reasons than one. No fella can soak up all that whisky, not even Baldy, without repercussions. I'm telling you, that fella's going to go berserk!'

'Will I go back in again?'

'Oh, no!' Mrs Gordon and Catriona cried out in unison.

'Jimmy, son, you've done more than your share with Baldy.'

'Yes,' Catriona agreed. 'There's plenty of people in there and they're all staying until after . . . until – until morning.'

'Melvin says you've to go downstairs in case the wee fella wakes up,' said Sandy.

'I'll go doon with you, hen,' Lexy offered from the doorway where she was wiping her nose on one of Jimmy's big white hankies supplied by Mrs Gordon for the purpose. 'I'll stay the rest of the night with you till Melvin comes.'

'Thank you. You're very kind.'

Where was the dream and where the reality?

Surely she belonged with the man who was now walking with her in silence to the door? Surely she had known him all her life? He was the fulfilment of her need, he was the braver, better part of her.

Yet she was married to another man – a stranger.

At first, going down the dark stairs with Lexy sniffling at her side, she felt dazed. Then came the bitterness to kick and struggle angrily against fate.

She opened the door of her house and stepped into the hall – and hated it; hated the hard gleaming polish of the floor that both she and Fergus had been warned so often not to tread on. Little remnants of rugs lay like stepping stones between the front door and all the other doors.

She hated the bedrooms where the bed-ends, the top of the wardrobe and the skirting board had to be rubbed and rubbed and polished and polished. She hated the bathroom where Melvin was now insisting the high-painted walls ought to be waxed to preserve them against steam.

Most of all she hated the sitting-room, Melvin's pride and joy, with its pastel coloured Indian carpet that was an agony to keep clean and the pale gold standard-lamp on which she dared not allow dust to settle and the ornate brass front and fender on the fireplace over which, on Melvin's instructions, she had spent many back-breaking, sweating and wasteful hours.

Life was so short. Surely, there were better ways to spend it?

She led Lexy into the kitchen and flicked on the light. Every surface glittered and gleamed, not a speck of dust, not a crumb, could be seen. Not one hair on the fireside rug was out of place, not one cushion dented.

Lexy's sniffles stopped. Uneasily she sat down on the edge of a seat, uncomfortably she stared around.

She's longing to light up a cigarette, Catriona thought,

but she's afraid to dirty the place or desecrate that brassoed ashtray.

Then it occurred to her that she was afraid, too, the realization made her hate herself with such intensity that she felt physically sick.

'Ohi, I hope Jimmy doesn't go in to Baldy again.' Lexy worriedly nibbled at her lip. 'He's terrible, isn't he? I mean, he's a lovely fella.' She gave a big sigh. 'But, ohi, he's terrible too. I mean to say – isn't he?'

'Can I make you a cup of tea?' Catriona managed.

'Oh, in the name of the wee man! I've never stopped drinking tea all day and half the night. I couldn't drink another drop, even if you paid me. If I drink any more I'd be wetting my pants!'

'Well, come on through to the sitting-room. There isn't a fire lit there either but at least there's the electric fire. It'll heat us up.'

Through in the sitting-room she switched on all the lights and the fire and drew a couple of chairs in nearer. They sat for a long time, staring at the fire and at the slow but relentlessly moving hand of the clock.

Catriona had begun to shiver, whether with cold or fear or with hatred or with all three she no longer knew nor cared.

'I've never been up this late before except at Hogmanay, have you, eh?' Lexy said eventually.

Catriona shook her head.

'Ohi – I'm gaspin' for a fag!'

'Go ahead then, have one.'

'Are you sure you don't mind, hen?'

'No, not me. Make yourself at home. You're welcome.'

'Oh, ta! You're a pal!' Lexy dived into one of her pockets and brought out cigarettes and matches. 'Here, try one yourself, hen. It'll steady your nerves. I mean to say – what with one thing and another!' She rolled her eyes. 'I don't know about you but I'm nearly off my head, so I am!'

Catriona hesitated only a moment before taking a cigarette and accepting the light Lexy gave her.

She coughed and spluttered after the first couple of puffs but soon settled down to find the cigarette strangely comforting. She liked the feel of it between her fingers. It gave her something to cling on to. She enjoyed the sucking sensation, and the breathing in, and the breathing out, like huge shuddering sighs of relief.

They smoked in silence, and when one cigarette was finished they each lit another, and another. They tried not to listen to the clock ticking Sarah's life away.

'Here!' Lexy cried out, for the first time noticing the shivering and the white angry face. 'Are you feeling all right?'

Catriona was saved from answering by the sound of Melvin's key in the door.

They both got up and pushed back their chairs.

'Are you sure you won't have a cup of tea, Lexy?'

'No! Thanks all the same, hen, but I'd rather run back upstairs to my Jimmy!'

Catriona's heart wept hard stones.

'What the hell!' After Lexy had gone Melvin saw Catriona smoking. 'Put that thing in the bucket. You're not going to start that filthy habit in my house. You're not going to go around dropping ash on my good carpets or my good linoleum; and that's that!'

'No, that's not that! You smoke! Why shouldn't I smoke?'

'What? What did you say?'

'Oh, shut up!' Catriona shot the words at him then hurled the still-lighted cigarette into the spotless hearth with such force it bounced out again and landed on the Indian carpet.

With a howl of rage and fear for the damage it might cause, Melvin pounced on the cigarette and with garbled oaths and burning fingers he at last managed to extinguish it in the nearest receptacle which happened to be a fancy and much-prized fruit-bowl, one of the wedding presents he and Betty had received.

'Now look what you've done, you stupid fool!' he bawled. 'Look at my good fruit-bowl.'

'What *I've* done? I never touched your horrible fruit-bowl. You put it there, not me.'

'You put it on my good carpet. What did you expect me to do? Leave it lying there to burn a hole – a hole in my good carpet?'

'Oh, shut up, shut up, shut up! Talk about jumping from the frying-pan into the fire. My mother's one extreme, you're the other, and the irony of it is – you're worse! I'm so sick of hearing about your furniture and your linoleum and your carpets. I don't care if this whole place burns to a cinder and all your precious possessions in it!'

Melvin surveyed her, his stocky legs wide, his broad hands digging into his waist. 'Now I know exactly what kind of horror I've the misfortune to marry.'

'That makes two of us,' she retorted bitterly. 'I certainly know what kind of horror you are now.'

'I've been a good husband to you,' he shouted indignantly. 'I've given you a good home.'

'This isn't my home. It isn't a home at all.'

'Look at all the things I've provided you with. I've even made you a present of Betty's clothes! What more could any man give you?'

She shook her head, the sickness and the shivering swamping her again.

'Nothing, nothing. I'm sorry for everything I said.'

'A fat lot you gave me! You'd neither a stitch to your back nor a penny to your name.'

'I said I was sorry.'

'You ought to be down on your knees to me in gratitude.'

Her eyes flashed fired and hatred at him again.

'You'd like that, wouldn't you?'

'What the hell are we standing here in the middle of the night arguing for?' He suddenly scratched his moustache as if a better idea had occurred to him. 'I'm away through to the kitchen and after I do my press-ups I'll show you the way to express your gratitude! Come on! Don't just stand there!' He chortled. 'There's been enough hot stuff on this carpet for one night. Let's see what you can do in the kitchen!'

Chapter 23

The room was heavy-clouded with smoke and thick with whisky fumes.

Sandy had dozed off in one of the chairs beside the fire. Tam sat nodding opposite, short legs splayed out, big muscly arms crossed over his chest.

Men were draped, in drunken stupors, over different chairs.

Francis and Eddie MacMahon and wee Andy Tucker were propping each other up on the settee. Josy McWhirter's cherubic face had flopped down and hung by his fat chin on the edge of the table.

Only Rab and Baldy were awake and still steadily drinking; Baldy with his sleeves rolled up and his unbuttoned shirt hanging open to the waist like a heavy-weight ju-jitsu expert or a huge all-in wrestler, and Rab leaning back, dark-jawed and big-boned, absently sliding his glass backwards and forwards across the table from one hand to the other.

Nobody noticed that Baldy had stopped speaking and was staring across at the window and at the clock on the mantelpiece, then at the window, then at the clock, then at the window.

Until suddenly a low snarl began to raise the hairs on the back of everyone's neck and by the time the snarl had increased in volume and menace to become first a growl as Baldy reeled from the table, then a terrifying gorilla-like roar, everyone was on their feet, restraining hands outstretched at the ready, mouths open in an agonized panic-stricken search to find the right words.

Baldy shot both arms up and sent the table, bottles, glasses, ashtrays, spluttering all over the room.

'The bloody cowards!' His big chest expanded. 'The bastards!' Lunging at the mantelpiece, despite the half-dozen or so men hanging on to him, he grabbed the clock and sent it hurtling through the window with an explosion, then a tinkling of broken glass. A couple of white 'wally dugs' flew through the air next.

'Baldy!' Rab shouted as one of the china dogs hit the wall. He fought to twist Baldy's tree-trunk arm behind his back. 'You're wrecking your house, man!'

Baldy heaved round and sent Rab flying. 'What bloody good is a house to me now!'

Rab struggled to his feet again.

'Sarah wouldn't want you to be getting into a state like this.'

'Aye!' Tam cried. 'That lassie worshipped the ground you walked on. Think of her!'

'I am thinking of her, you stupid fool!' He yelled all the louder but tears were spurting, streaming down. 'I promised I wouldn't let any of them bastards touch her. She's my wife!'

After she had recovered from the shock of what the Lord Provost had told her, Sarah refused to believe it. Not that she had the temerity to suppose anyone as important as the Lord Provost would tell a deliberate lie, but because his words and the words of the learned judge – '. . . you will be hanged by the neck until you are dead . . .' – were beyond her realm of comprehension, had no place, did not belong in the world where the authorities and the powers-that-be had always commanded her secret awe, respect and admiration. She put the whole thing down to some sort of stupid mistake on her part. 'Sarah, hen,' she told herself, 'ye've picked them up wrong.'

Yet in the deeper lonelier layers of her mind she could

not convince herself. She had done a terrible thing and she would be punished terribly. The thought came rushing in on a white horse of fear but was beaten back again.

It was the idea of respectable folk (the Baillies were going to be there) calmly walking her along and putting a rope round her neck that confused her. Even the holy yin seemed to think it was all right.

So it must be all right.

Yet she couldn't believe it.

But it was true.

The waves were surging in and in. And the cell was small. Nowhere to escape, nobody to turn to. She was sorry.

Sometimes the shame of having disgraced Baldy and the MacNairs and the street was too much to bear.

She couldn't sleep.

There had been dirty washing in the lobby press, and the furniture and all the ornaments were dusty.

If folk were coming in and out looking after Baldy they would see it and Baldy would get a showing up. She should have left the house clean and tidy.

Her cheeks burned.

Had she *really* seen her house for the last time; her cosy fire, her chair with the velvet cushion, her bonny china with the roses all around?

No, in her heart she knew that was impossible. Soon, she would be going home again.

Baldy would come in. He was a lad, her Baldy, but they'd always rubbed along that well together.

He had been good to her. Never once had he complained. And what had she done in return? What kind of wife had she been to him?

'Och, Baldy, lad, ah feel that ashamed!'

In the morning she would go down to old MacNair's. It was a lovely shop that. The best shop in Glasgow. Warm as toast and smelling just as tasty and always somebody ready to have a laugh and nice wee blether. Many a laugh she'd enjoyed in there.

No more mornings.

She felt frightened. It was morning now.

The city magistrates and the governor and the town clerk's deputy and the chief constable of Glasgow and the doctor and the holy yin were there.

It seemed truly terrible to be putting all these important folk to all this trouble. She fumbled with her cardigan and with fast-beating heart endeavoured to answer their questions with fitting politeness. She crinkled her face up and smiled apologetically round and round at them all.

It was a very serious and dignified procession and she tried to keep decently in step.

No more steps.

The waves came pounding over her. Horror was the scaffold. Terror was the instinctive need to keep alive.

Impossible to escape.

No time to bridge the hopeless gulf between her and her executioners.

The pain that had continuously dragged low down at her back and her abdomen flared into unbearable anguish, and at the last moment, before a man put the cap over her head, she felt grateful for the custom of making condemned women prisoners wear rubber underwear.

Fear beyond all measure. Darkness – and death long-drawn-out.

There was only one thing left that Jimmy could do, and that was to go to Duke Street Prison.

He knew his being there, standing outside the big bleak wall in the early morning with the collar of his jacket turned up and his hands dug deep into his pockets, could do nothing to stop what was going to happen to Sarah. But he imagined she needed a friend close by and this was as close as he could get.

His eyes, black-shadowed in an unshaven face, stared up at the prison.

At one time, when an execution took place a man could be seen hoisting a square black flag on a flagstaff at the western end of the prison roof while the prison bell tolled a dismal announcement that the criminal had paid the penalty.

Now there was only the posting of a notice on the front wall.

No notice had been posted yet. He leaned against the wall and closed his eyes.

He wondered if there was a God. He had waded through the writings of Thomas Paine and other atheists and sceptics. He had come across some shocking atrocities in his reading about the history of the church.

All this weighed heavily against the existence of a deity, his mind tried to tell him. Still, in his heart he was not convinced. There was such bitterness, such derision in so many of the atheistic books and pamphlets. He wondered why they got so worked up about something they did not believe in.

As far as the church and some of the worst parts of its history were concerned, it seemed more reasonable to blame the *men* who had perpetrated the atrocities in God's name rather than God.

One had, he decided, to go back to the root of the matter. A Christian meant a follower of and a believer in Christ.

Did he believe in Jesus Christ?

He had no time for droning-voiced hypocrites who hid behind dog-collars. Or all the pomp and jewelled crowns and expensive robes and impressive trumpeting of all the churches in the world put together.

But what had they got to do with Christ? The Christ who was a tradesman – a carpenter. The Christ who, when He went into the temple and found those who were selling oxen and sheep and pigeons, and the money-changers at their business, made a whip of cords and drove them all, with their sheep and oxen, out of the temple, and poured out the coins of the money-changers and overturned their tables.

It needed only a little imagination to see that it took a lot of nerve to do things like that, or a very strong character – or something more.

The miracle was that, despite the difficulties of translation, of words themselves as a means of communication and the human limitations of the men who recorded the books of the New Testament, in spite of the changing customs, despite men's varying interpretations of Him, the spirit and the reality of Christ had survived all down through the ages.

Yes, he believed in Him!

A creaking, scraping sound alerted his attention, made his eyes dart round, his chest tighten, his breathing become difficult.

A prison officer had opened the gate and stepped out, a piece of paper in his hand.

No, Jimmy thought. No! He stared helplessly, the words of the notice drumming in his mind and building up to pain in his chest, cramping his shoulder and making him feel breathless and more breathless.

No . . . No . . .

He wandered away, climbed on a tramcar and trundled back to Clydend, his face a sickly putty colour, his whole attention now focused on the seemingly insurmountable difficulties of reaching the quietness of home, the relaxation of bed. Gasping, fighting to keep calm, he got off the car at the Main Road a few steps away from Dessie Street. The street was strewn with glass and broken pieces of pottery.

His feet crunched and clattered and stumbled over them. Into the close. Stop to lean against the coolness of the wall. On to the stairs, the banister hard and strong under his hand pulling him up.

Pain knifing him.

The first landing reached. Rest again, head rolling against wall. Pray for quietness to help keep calm. He wanted to live.

Noise swelled and reverberated around him like a riotous tenement symphony. Baldy shouting and sobbing. Rab and Tam and Sandy and a cacophony of other voices vying with each other in loudness.

Then from somewhere behind the door near which he had propped himself came another sound.

A girl was screaming.

Chapter 24

Catriona followed Melvin from the front room, across the hall and into the kitchen like an obedient child. Outwardly silent and subdued, she reeled inside frantic for escape. She had been up all night imagining and dreading the hour of Sarah's execution. The hour was near. Now she longed for peace of mind to pray. She needed every last ounce of energy to plead with God to forgive Sarah in case more punishment awaited her after death. She wanted to beg Him for mercy. Somehow she had to gather the courage to say: '"Thy will be done", but if it is Your will that Sarah should die, please comfort her!'

She had to fight down revulsion and bitterness and hatred and ask His forgiveness for Sarah's executioners because it said in the Lord's prayer, 'Forgive us our trespasses as we forgive them that trespass against us.'

Before she dared open her mind to God it had to be very carefully prepared because He could see in every dark and secret corner. She had to be still and quiet, in awe and reverence.

Instead she was teetering on the verge of panic.

Melvin could not expect sex now. Not now! It was impossible. It could not be right. Surely it was obscenity to the point of madness to even think of sexual intercourse at a time like this?

Somehow her legs conveyed her into the kitchen where she had to hold on to the back of a chair for support.

Melvin was too busy to notice.

He stripped off his jacket, then his shirt and, naked to the waist, began limbering up. Muscles and veins bulged like balloons at bursting point as he jerked himself into different poses. Grunting, he grabbed his wrists and made his chest puff high like a woman's. He dropped his arms and made his shoulders swell up like the hunchback of Notre-Dame. He whipped round, arms held high, fists curled, and snorted over his shoulder at her.

'That back development's out of this world, you know. It has to be seen to be believed!'

He faced her again, hand clamped on waist, and began high-stepping up and down. He dropped low to squat on his heels and bounced to his toes again. He finished off by lying on his stomach and doing a few press-ups. Then he rolled around, gave his moustache a good scratch and grinned up at her.

'Come on then, darlin'! Let's see what you can do!'

She could hear Baldy upstairs, and the other men, and the thumping and the crashing. The world was noisily disintegrating. The child might waken at any minute and be frightened.

Was Sarah frightened now?

'Come on!' One of Melvin's broad hands groped up her skirt. 'Let's see you!'

She screamed – jerky, ceiling-pitched, staccato bursts, piercing. She clawed for the door, his hands imprisoning her.

The quick patter of feet in the hall and Fergus shouting.

The hands releasing. Escape. Into the hall, fight with the handle of the front door. The landing. Jimmy in the shadows. In exquisite gratitude she clung to the Harris tweed jacket, moved her face and lips in the warm hollow of his neck, prayed to melt safely inside him, be one with him, protected by his gentleness and understanding.

Suddenly love alerted her. All thoughts of herself forgotten she stared up at Jimmy's face.

'Jimmy, love . . . Lean on me . . . I'll take you home, I'll help you upstairs.'

He shook his head.

'Oh, Jimmy!'

With desperate, fumbling fingers, she loosened his tie and unbuttoned his shirt.

'What the hell . . .?' Melvin's iron grip wrenched her away. 'Right on my doorstep, too! I knew he was an impertinent bastard but this is bloody ridiculous!'

Jimmy twisted against the wall, his head to one side.

Panic swirled round Catriona again.

'He's ill! Can't you see? Are you always blind? Oh, please, please, Melvin – help him!'

'I know him,' Melvin sneered. 'I've known him a lot longer than you. He's been to the prison. He's been working himself into a stupid tizzy over a useless dirty slut like Sarah Fowler. I'll deal with you at work tomorrow, Gordon. Right now I've a thing or two to say to my wife!'

The door crashed shut and they were in the hall and she was aching to kill him!

Only for Jimmy's sake did she pin down her voice and emotions.

'Go get a doctor. Please, please, oh, please, Melvin! I'll do anything. I'll promise. I'll never speak to Jimmy again. Only do something, anything to help him!'

'Watch where you're going. You'll dirty the linoleum!' Melvin raised his voice indignantly. 'Walk on the rugs. What do you think I put rugs on this floor for? I went to a lot of bother to get those rugs and place them just right to protect the good linoleum.'

'Dirty the linoleum? You're worrying about dirtying the linoleum?' She laughed with hysteria. 'You'd think there was nothing more to life.'

'But there isn't!' Melvin said, genuinely astonished at her ignorance. 'That's all life is – a fight against dirt.'

Darkness billowed around her. Wildly she struggled against the black cloth.

She fought with her fists, her feet, her teeth, her nails, all the strength that was in her, but Melvin's muscles bulged, proud of their superior strength, and the black cloth snaked around her, smothering her, whirling her down . . .

Consciousness returned and it seemed that she had never stopped struggling.

Only now she was in the bedroom, and she was trapped in a tunnel of blankets and her hair was flopping from one side to the other of a lumpy pillow.

'Take it easy,' Melvin was saying. 'Just take it easy, OK?' Reaching over he heaved her into a sitting position. 'The doctor's been and had a look at you. He's upstairs now but he'll pop in again later.'

'Jimmy!' She flung the blankets aside and would have been out of bed but Melvin's iron arms restrained her like the bars of a prison.

His face acquired a solemn expression. 'It's too late.' He gave a long serious sigh. 'He wouldn't do as he was told, you see. We were always telling him – his mother, Sandy, Lexy, your father, Tam, and nobody more than me. Take it easy, we all kept warning him, don't get so worked up about everything – keep calm – don't bother – why worry? But we just couldn't do anything with him. He was always sticking his neck out; always ruffling himself up, and other folk, too.'

'Oh, no.' Catriona shook her head.

'Yes, he was. I knew him longer than you. He was always on about something or somebody. He even had the nerve to argue with the old man. They were always arguing the toss. This'll be a terrible shock for the old man. He liked him, you know. Och, to hell, I liked the fella too, even though he made a bloody nuisance of himself.'

'Jimmy's not dead. You said he was only upset.'

Melvin's face darkened with annoyance.

'I told you he'd been to the prison and got himself all worked up and I was right. How was I to know he'd gone too far and was going to die on my doorstep? I wouldn't have known yet, but Mata Hari across the landing was spying through her keyhole. She saw him drop and came hirpling straight in to tell me.'

'Jimmy's dead?'

'That'll be another night and day the place will be shut,' Melvin said. 'And he'll have a big funeral. Here, I bet the old man'll shut the shop on the day of the funeral as well. Jumpin' Jesus, that'll be three days.'

The veil of romantic fiction, the fairy-tales, all the comforting imaginings she had always hopefully clung to ripped away. Through death, she saw life.

'Oh, well!' Melvin scratched his moustache. 'As long as I get my wages!'

No fairy godmother. No Sir Galahad. No ship coming in. No last minute happy ending. Nothing round the corner.

'I'll need all the money I can lay my hands on now that you're pregnant.'

'Pregnant!'

Life went on. People went on, generation after generation, countless millions. Poseurs behind masks, duping themselves with self-importance, busy with minutiae.

'I don't suppose you even know what the word pregnant means. You don't know nothing, darlin'!' Melvin got up, stretching his muscles and laughing.

Life was the survival of the fittest.

Life was Glasgow, tough, harsh, complex, warm with humanity, with generous helping hands, with caring in abundance.

It was the caring that mattered.

'I'm learning,' she said.